Plum Creek Valley

Plum Creek Valley

By
Rose S. Bell

Copyright © 2004 by Rose S. Bell.
Printed in the United States. All rights reserved.

ISBN 1-58597-271-1

Library of Congress Control Number: 2004093681

A division of Squire Publishers, Inc.
4500 College Blvd.
Leawood, KS 66211
1/888/888-7696
www.leatherspublishing.com

Prologue

Plum Creek Valley is a fictional name and location in the Deep South. Its first two characters were slave children whose only daughter marries the love of her life, and she was also the love of his life. At the time of their marriage, the young woman, Sarah, was 19 years old, and the young man, Jason, was a very mature 23 years old. They had both been reared in homes where the parents wanted them to move with honesty and integrity against the waves of slavery. This concept, though a wonderfully meaningful and beautiful one, was easier said than done.

Fourteen third-generation children of the two slave children were born to Sarah and Jason. These third-generation children were as carefully reared as their parents had been. They started to reproduce the fourth generation. Looking back and looking around at the results of slavery meant for these people a strong will to overcome the evils that slavery had brought to colored people in Plum Creek Valley of the Deep South.

These children were taught to love their parents, to love God, to do honest work, to love and highly regard reading, learning and getting educated. All of these things would aid in the development of the people they could now become, and that they now meant to become.

Those first two characters or slave children, Lawrence and Mattie Newsom, saw much in their span of years since 1858 and 1860. They witnessed ex-slaves' families vote, use telephones, ride in motor cars, use air travel, enter World War I, The Great Influenza Epidemic, The Great Depression, Ku Klux Klan, use Madam C. J. Walker's Hair Care, live with Jim Crow laws, attend colleges, write books, use conventional acceptable methods of birth control, establish the powerful NAACP, etc. They also witnessed sharecropping.

The love between Sarah Newsom Solley and Jason Solley not only prevailed, but became stronger and stronger as the years went by. Their unconditional love permeated their 14 children's lives, and their children's children's lives. They were very demanding of their children's talents — demanding in such a way that it was appreciated by the children as they grew up doing what they had striven to do.

It is hoped by this author that many students all over these United States of America, and possibly beyond, will get the opportunity to read and understand the real message of this book. For older adults it might provide not only reminiscence, but a recognition of hopes and dreams being fulfilled for Negroes and whites alike in America.

Any resemblance of the fictional characters of Plum Creek Valley to anyone living or dead is purely coincidental. They are products of this author's imagination.

Contents

Plum Creek Valley
    Lawrence Newsom b. 1858, Mattie b. 1860, Sarah b. 1879 1

Sarah, 1894 11

Jason and Sarah 28

New Beginning 31

The True Story Continues 37

Sarah's Wedding 42

Lawrence 48

The Solley Family Living 53

Aunt Pearl's Visit and Voting Rights for Colored People 61

President McKinley's Assassination 65

Third Generation of Slave-Born Children: Work, Church,
    School, and the Meaning of Freedom 68

One-Room School and a Good Teacher, Miss Blakeman 80

Cotton Picking and Home-Schooling 85

Questions and Answers about Sharecropping 90

World War I 95

1918 Influenza Epidemic 98

Solley Children 100

Ku Klux Klan 105

A Well-Respected Colored Man 108

Susan 111

Nona's Fella 114

The Bakers	116
Nona, Louise, Mindy	119
Jim	124
Hazel, Ray, Gerald, Charley, and Jim Crow Laws	126
Sarah and Nona and Babies	132
Fishing	135
Using the Land	139
NAACP	141
Madam C.J. Walker's Hair Care	143
Ray, Charley, John, Mark and Hazel	150
Jason, Sarah and a New Suit	152
Sarah's Eastern Star Meeting	168
Sophie	175
Claude and Edward	179
Canning and Syrup Making	181
The Great Depression	183
Jason, Claude and Edward	185
Joe Jr., Sophie, Claude, Edward	190
Fall 1939	194
The Sullivan Murder Case	208
New Year, New Telephone, Travel Time	215

Plum Creek Valley
Lawrence Newsom b. 1858, Mattie b. 1860, Sarah b. 1879

In this part of the country there were many who struggled to make a place for themselves and their families so soon after Lee surrendered to Grant in 1865. By the end of the century some felt that they could see more than a glimmer of light toward the end of the tunnel. Others wondered if life after slavery would ever be as bright and carefree as they had dreamed it would be. Sarah Newsom was an only child born 1879 exactly 14 years after the end of the Civil War. Sarah might have been a "spoiled brat" if she had not had so many responsibilities, so many chores, so much natural ambition, and talents to live with.

Plum Creek Valley consisted mostly of farmland, pastures and wooded areas. Being the only child of a colored farmer meant that Sarah, very early in her life, learned to plant seeds, hoe cotton, pick cotton, pick peas, beans, gather free-growing plums, and many other farming chores outside the house. Yet there were equally as many things to learn to do inside the house and yard. There was milk from the cows to be churned so that butter and buttermilk could be made to complete the meals, and also to be taken into town and peddled for extra money, especially in winter.

The cistern in the corner of the front yard usually furnished sufficient water supply for the family, but during the dry season rain water sometimes became too low in the cistern, causing the need for water to be supplemented from the natural spring which was some distance up the road past the mailbox. This meant that water could be hauled with the wagon and barrels, or if the need was most urgent and the mules and wagon were not available, water had to be brought up by water pails or empty molasses buckets by hand.

Sarah learned to wash dishes, cook, churn the milk, sew, sweep and scour the wooden floors while still a very young gal. Washing the dishes meant first heating the water in the black iron kettle and pot (enough to wash (with the same lye soap that was used to do the family wash). After the dishes were all washed, they were scalded with very hot water in a second pan, dried and put in the safe (a mobile cabinet of sorts) until the next meal.

An old second-hand sewing machine was operated by treading with the foot on the pedal while guiding the garment under the threaded needle. Many times Sarah had to first rip an old second-hand garment apart and cut it down to her size. Mattie, her ma, who seemed to know how to do just about everything, taught her how to remake these used clothes which were given to them by Mrs. Kelly and Mrs. Clark who lived in town. Once in a while the old clothes did not need remaking, and that left more time for piecing quilts, doing the vegetable garden or the flower yard. Saving time was important.

Mattie and Lawrence were very proud of their little gal who learned to join in their singing around the farm and home. "Swing Low, Sweet Chariot," "We'll understand It Better Bye and Bye," "Close to Thee," etc. were just some of the family singing that seemed to help ease the burden of work. Sarah could not only carry a tune, but she could lead without being self-conscious at church. In fact, she did so well that many of the church members, both old and young, depended on her to help them carry the tunes without the benefit of a piano. Pianos came with a cost that poor, still newly freed people rarely had. Even when a piano was occasionally given to a colored church, there was the problem of playing the notes. A few people could play some tunes by ear. Other than those piano lessons had to be taught and learned. That, of course, required money and time.

Sarah always secretly hated to cook. Even though it was a natural chore to learn for a post-Civil-War, post-slavery young colored girl. She almost always burned something (the bread got too brown or black, the dry peas cooked not quite enough, too much salt, the salt port didn't cook long enough before she put in the fresh green black-eye peas from the field, or something, something just not quite right! Why couldn't she cook better? She was going to have to ask Ma to show her how to do a better job in the kitchen rather than criticizing her. Her ma thought she was doing too much day dreaming while cooking food. She would tell Sarah, "Gal, you got to get yo' mind on what you doing. No man gonna wanta gal who ca' cook a good meal for him after he work like a horse all day!" Even though her feelings would be hurt, Sarah did not improve her cooking skills until her pa stepped in and rather shyly but firmly patted her on the shoulder and said that there would be a young man out there somewhere who would love her for all of her other good things and would be patient for her cooking to improve. He asked Sarah to just try a little more to watch the food, while knowing that her cooking would get better.

After that little speech of Pa's, Ma stood up at the table

and clapped her hands for him. Then she did the same for her daughter, admitting that she had not been as patient as she should have been. Sarah felt almost rejuvenated after that. She became more determined to keep her mind on cooking while cooking. Slowly but surely, her food became a little bit better. She never cooked as well as she could can fruits and vegetables. She never cooked as well as she could sew, make quilts, make a flower yard or sing, but her cooking was good enough to be eaten and nobody has to do everything good, she thought to herself. The best thing of all was that Mattie stopped talking her cooking down and began to say, "Gal, yo' cooking can be eat now."

Lawrence was always happy when his family was doing as well as they could under the circumstances. He sat after dinner reading just a little and mostly thinking about Mattie — how soft, and cuddly and sweet she could be when things quieted down after day's work came to an end. The household was an early rising one. Therefore, nobody went to bed very, very late. He touched Mattie's titties and then he patted her buttocks with a very light hand while Sarah was studying her arithmetic and spelling lessons. She had asked him to call her spelling words out to see that she missed none. She loved to be able to do all of her arithmetic problems.

School terms were quite short in some of the rural colored schools — three to five months instead of the eight or nine for many white schools. Sarah's school averaged three to five months. One year there was no money for the school. There was what some called a "Subscription School" because a teacher who accepted a sort of pay-in-kind taught the very short term. The parents gave pay other than cash. They were just that anxious for their younguns to get an education. Even though the colored schools many times found themselves being supplied with used books, it was better than the alternatives. At least colored children now had access to schools. The short school terms were usually divided into two parts; one part started in late fall after all the crops were gathered, and the cotton, peas, peanuts, corn and such had been safely brought in from the fields. It was now time for young colored field workers to turn into "school chillun." The words "school chillun" was used much more frequently than students. The second short part of the short school year was perhaps midsummer after the field crops were "laid by" and the field hands were no longer needed in the fields for a few weeks. It was not the most ideal way to get educated; however, it meant "getting educated." It was learning to read, write, do figures and spell long words, as well as short ones (Pennsylvania, Mississippi, extraordinary, etc.

Sarah learned to read much better than either her ma, Mattie, or her pa, Lawrence, because neither of them had come far enough beyond slavery's end to be the kind of readers that their young gal was. Yet, Sarah had only been able to complete fifth grade. When she had asked her pa to call out her spelling words, she was careful to see that he knew how to pronounce the words on the list that she gave him to call from. In this way, he was also learning. His reading had been limited. He wanted Sarah to keep readin', writin' and doing figures. Many colored men and women who had been born into slavery as had Lawrence and Mattie could read very little or not all by the time their children were fourth or fifth grade. Lawrence had been born about 1858 and Mattie about 1860. They were far more familiar with their hoes, plows, axes and saws than they were with ABCs, words and numbers on a page. However, both could do somewhat limited reading, for which they were very proud of themselves and proud of each other.

Mrs. Amy Kelly and Mrs. Nora Clark, who sent their weekly wash each Monday to Mattie, would line their dirty clothes baskets with their old newspapers and their discarded magazines. These discarded reading materials would be welcomed by the Newsoms because here was another opportunity for reading whatever was of interest and whatever they had time to learn something more from. Between Mrs. Clark, and Mrs. Kelly, the Newsom family was kept pretty busy with washings, ironing and reading. All they needed was more time, time, time.

On Monday mornings Lawrence would drive the buggy into town to pick up the clothes. No need to waste a whole wagon and two mules to carry into town a few eggs, butter and milk to sell and then return with two baskets of dirty clothes to be washed and ironed, he reckoned. Therefore, the buggy was enough.

As Lawrence's mule walked briskly down the narrow road near the creek, Lawrence looked out across plowed and freshly planted fields. He drove along thinking, thinking, and trying hard to imagine what the new situation would be like if that Civil War Special Field Order #15 in 1865 had gone into full effect for colored farmers. It had to do with a Freedmen Protection; a kind of proposal sometimes referred to as "40 Acres and a Mule" for newly freedmen. One thing he knew for sure was that he and some people he knew did not get a "piece of that pie." His farmland had not come to him like that. Some white men had good hearts and wanted to clear and clean their conscience; they helped some colored men get a start, especially if they showed promise. As the mule neared the creek, Lawrence looked down into the rushing water. As he started to cross the bridge, his eyes caught the sight of flirting fish. He thought how he'd like to just go fishing today.

But no, there was not time for that today or anything else except what he did Monday mornings. He had to haul the clothes home.

Ma and Sarah would have drawn up water for the big black wash pot near the cistern, and for the tubs of water to wash and rinse the clothes which had to be done up exactly right. Mrs. Clark's husband was a preacher, and their son John was following in his footsteps. Every Sunday both the older man and the young man wore their white shirts that must be starched and ironed. When they visited the sick or had a funeral to service, that meant the same kind of dress as on Sunday. They never could wear the same shirt twice before washing again. Being the preacher's wife meant that Mrs. Clark had starched and ironed dresses for every day of the week.

Mrs. Kelly's wash did not have to be done with quite so much painstaking. She had five children with no special clothes washing and ironing needs. Yet everything had to be ironed, for there was no drip-dry miracle clothes during the late 1800s. The flat iron or "smoothing" iron, as it was sometimes called, had to be heated on top of the stove or in the fireplace or outside on top of hot coals. Mr. Kelly did not seem to have any real concerns about his clothes. They were presentable for him to supervise the packinghouse on the edge of Old Town. The word around town, and in the rural areas, too, was that Mr. Kelly was a fair man. He saw to it that his work hands got full pay for all the work they had done. There were no shortages in their pay envelopes. Since those pay envelopes represented a whole lot of work and had to pay for a whole lot of living, this was very important. However, hard work was expected of the work hands.

Mattie had gone out to look down the road several times to see if Lawrence was in sight. She was getting impatient to get those clothes in the water and on the line. She didn't want to go start in the garden because there was hoeing, weed pulling and bean poles to stick in the ground. When she got into that, she hated to stop and have to start again. She wanted to get the clothes dried while she was pretty sure of a sunny morning. Rain had been predicted for later. Thank God, the old buggy was pulling up to the barn gate at last.

It was near eight, and if all went well the clothes would be dry by noon and could be ironed in the afternoon. The next morning they would be returned to town. With that over, Mattie and Sarah could put their minds on their own work because it would still be waiting for them. Yes, Lawrence was a little slow today.

Lawrence had been taught from a very young boy to say, "Yes, ma'am; no, ma'am; please, ma'am; thank you, ma'am; and you welcome, ma'am" to all white ladies, young and old. He also knew better than to be too friendly and grin at white women. His pa and ma had told him that colored boys could get in a heap of trouble by doing that. He'd always been too scared to disobey because he'd heard some bad scary tales about nigger boys being hung up on a tree limb by the neck. Some folks called it lynching. He sure didn't want to die before the Good Lawd got ready for him to die; and dying that way sho 'nuf would not be God's doing — not the God he'd learned about in his church, not the God he prayed to with Ma and Sarah before each meal and again at bedtime. No, no, no!

When Lawrence had picked the clothes up that morning, two things unusual had delayed him just a little. A dead fox was right in the wheel rut of the very narrow road. Therefore, the removal of the fox was the only thing to do, and this took a little more time than it should have because he dragged the dead fox quite a distance from the road. Soon it would start to stink, and the farther away the better for everybody coming along here.

The second delay happened at Mrs. Kelly's house when he went around to the back door as usual to pick up the clothes basket. Mrs. Kelly was not feeling well, and Miss Miriam, the oldest girl, answered the knock. Instead of just saying good morning and pushing the clothes basket toward him with her foot, she smiled at him with all of her pretty perfect white teeth. The smile was innocent, and he was caught off guard when she said, "Take a minute or two and eat two or three buttered biscuits and honey with a cup of coffee. You surely didn't have breakfast yet," She smiled again very nicely. He had been caught off guard but not too much, because he remembered just in time not to grin at her. He was afraid that his smile might be thought as grinning at this pretty white girl and, oh, he could be in a heap of trouble. He said, "No, thank you ma'am. I gots to get back home with these clothes." She was not to be dissuaded and continued with, "I've fried some side meat, so take just a little with your biscuits." He didn't want to displease her because that could cause trouble, maybe. Lawrence ate quickly and did a whole lot of "Thank you, ma'am, Miss Miriam." Then he quickly thought to add, "I sho' hopes Miss Kelly will be all right right away." Now he was going to be late getting home for sure. Mattie and Sarah would be ready for the clothes. No harm had been done, but he had to drive old Buck fast to try to make up for losing time twice on this trip to pick up the two washes.

He didn't need a second breakfast, and so went straight to the barn. He found himself thinking again as he'd done numerous times about how nice it would be if he had a son. His gal child had always been a joy. She was sho' more of a ma's gal than a pa's. She was a tomboy though (climbing trees with her cousins, riding bushes down horsey-horse, running and jumping over rail fences). She even helped me twice complete a rail fence that I was building for a watermelon patch and a butterbean patch, he thought.

Lawrence thought of his brother's sons who were all older than his Sarah. They could plough the fields, saw down the trees to make wood for the cooking stove, the heater stove and the fireplace. They also sawed logs to be split into rails. Making wooden rails from trees was real hard work, but it did provide fences without money.

Lawrence's nephews would swap work with him by doing some of his farm jobs that he had no boys to do, and Mattie and Sarah would come to their farm with Lawrence to do things that they could to help. This was a good arrangement. Everyone got some help that was needed. Mattie and Sarah could chop cotton, pick peas, etc. Some of the colored women could pull a crosscut saw to cut up logs for firewood or anything else. Some of them could get behind a middle buster plow to guide it down the rows of corn or sugar cane while the mules stepped briskly to pull the plow. It was not an easy job for a woman. Lawrence forbade this.

Sarah, 1894

    Sarah had just celebrated her "Sweet Fifteen" birthday. In Mattie's house that birthday was named so because now she gave her permission for Sarah to "take company." Some of the gals around the area of Plum Creek Valley could start "taking company" at 14 and some not until 16, but when Mattie set her mind that something was right for her or her family, that was just what she did, by golly! This special birthday did not mean though, that now Sarah could go walking to town or through the wooded path to church or to the Fourth of July Picnic all by herself with her fella. They could, however, walk or ride in the wagon when others were going, too. If they wanted to hold hands, Mattie saw no harm in that. Just holding hands was not any harm.

    Mattie had been saying what she thought was the right thing to say to Sarah ever since the day her pa had sent her home from the field to tell ma to "fix her up" when Sarah was 12 because she had started to be a young woman. No, No, his little gal was not just a little gal anymore! They had been chopping the weeds and grass in the late spring sweet corn patch in the valley when Sarah felt something happening between her legs, and she knew that she did not have to go to the bushes to pee. Ma had not told her yet about the monthly period, because she, like many other colored women at that time, did not believe their little gals needed to know about such things until it was time. It was thought that if they were told "woman things" too soon, it might make them "fast." This meant they'd start thinking they be grown befo' time. Some of the mamas were a little bit shame to talk, but they knowed the day would come when they'd have to say to their little gals, "You don' started." Those were magical words for ma and child. They were not only magical, but so powerful.

The meaning of those three words did not stop immediately. The meaning was deep and the implications were far reaching, especially for little colored girls growing up poor in places like Plum Creek Valley. These simple-sounding words meant, "You ain't a little carefree gal no mo'. You can now have a baby just like yo' ma, but the difference is yo' ma is married to yo' pa. Do you hope for a better life for yo' baby than you have or do you mind if yo' baby has to work double most of the time? Working double meaning lots of things like working in yo' little house and barn and fields, then going over to work in that white lady's kitchen and bring her clothes to yo' house to wash. Sometimes you might only have a cistern in yo' little yard to supply the wash water. If it doesn't rain often for a while, you may have to tote the water from the natural spring in buckets or haul it in the wagon with barrels to the washing spot in yo' back yard. Working double also means ironing both yo' wash, as well as ironing the other wash or washes. If you wonder why you might not have a well instead of a cistern, it's not always as easy to get a deep well dug as it is to make a cistern which catches rain water. Well diggers cost money."

"You don' started," said by a colored ma to her young gal also meant, "You not only have started a monthly period, but started to be held responsible for your relationship with the boys, started to understand that you can never ever let a boy talk you into pulling yo' skirt up and pulling yo' bloomers down because he asked you to 'do it' for him. Instead, think of yourself. Think of not ever putting yourself in a place to be ostracized or completely disgraced and also displeasing the God who so lately delivered us colored folks from slavery. We shouldn't dishonor him by having babies before marriage. That is a mortal sin. The Bible teaches that 'doing it' with a boy before marriage is being a very bad girl. This could go on and on."

On the other hand, "You don' started" should mean beautiful and happy things can be in the future for you. You can meet the right fella after you have grown up and learned everything you should at school, and can now cook, wash, iron, make quilts, sew clothes, patch worn clothes, hoe cotton, pick cotton, etc., etc. It could mean that after seeing several fellas to court, you might choose one to be yo' husband. Then it will be time to have some babies, not befo'. No, not one minute befo' though!

Mattie had done her best to prepare her Sarah for the kind of life that was ahead of her. Yet deep in her heart she wanted Sarah's life to be easier than hers had been. She thought of going into the plum thickets picking up pails of succulent yellow tree-ripened plums, and then shaking the trees to make more plums fall so that she could fill her buckets. Some of them were used to make a plum cobbler, and others were carried into town to peddle to the white folks' houses. They would buy the plums, but Mattie never felt that they paid them enough for the picking up, the walking to town, and then peddling. Peddling was a fairly sure way to sell what you have, but one day was always different from the next. Some days the plums sold fast, some days took more walking up and down the dirt streets and knocking on the back doors. Finally all of the buckets were sold and they could usually start on the dirt road back home. Sometimes, however, if it were late enough for the general store to be open, they might stop in and buy a spool of white and a spool of black sewing thread, because there was always sewing of some kind waiting to be done at the day's end. The needle and thread were used more by coal oil lamp light than daylight, because after the outside work was done and the dishes washed it was time to finally sit down to the quilting, sewing, patching. This really could be a relaxing time of day, especially if it was started early enough to get into bed before late. That was always the aim, because whether they reached their beds on time or late they generally got up early. Days were long.

When school was in its late fall/winter term, Sarah did her schoolbooks work as soon as she milked a cow, brought in wood and maybe washed dishes. Sometimes Ma washed dishes so that Sarah could get to her schoolwork. Sometimes Sarah's best friend, Catherine Kelly, came over to spend Friday night. They were both the same age so they could talk, talk and giggle about their fellas. Both were decent, good, well-mannered girls. Both were allowed to take company at this time. Catherine's birthday had come in July and Sarah's had come in October. These two friends occasionally sat in the extra seat of Lawrence's and Mattie's wagon on Saturday afternoon as the four of them went to town. Going to town that way was a special fun trip (no clothes to pick up or to deliver after the washing, no plums to peddle, no eggs or butter to sell). Only a few necessary things were bought in town. It was a good wagon ride to just enjoy and see the trees, squirrels and birds. In town there were some familiar faces of friends doing the same thing (mostly looking and spending the nickel or dime which had been saved up just for such a time as this because it would not happen again soon).

Sarah shared her warm feeling about her beau, Jason Solley, with her friend. As usual, Catherine was all ears for when and whatever her friend cared to tell her about her fellas or the boys who showed that they would like to be. The two friends usually got along very well. They had much in common.

They agreed on many things, and that is why they were such devoted friends. They agreed that they should try as hard as they could to study their lessons for their one-room school, and to be courted by more than one fella before agreeing to get married no matter how much they liked him. They would not dishonor themselves, their families, their teacher, or their God who had brought them and their families out of slavery by getting weak enough to do bad things with boys. They felt very sorry for Annie McFadden who had let a boy get her "in the family way." She was not a bad girl. In fact, they saw nothing in Annie except a good girl who was "in trouble." To be "in trouble" was a saying that was so fitting because the situation was troublesome indeed for Annie. The boy, on the other hand, had the choice of completely denying that he had ever touched the girl, or admitting his part in all this and wanting to or agreeing to marry her. On the other hand, the boy could be forced by the gal's pa into a "shotgun" marriage. Catherine and Sarah quickly agreed that neither of them would ever want their fella to be forced to marry her. How shameful that would be! It could be quite humiliating and belittling! Annie McFadden's plight did sadden them both. What would become of her? They wished for her a good outcome.

Sarah's fella, Jason Solley, had some pretty stiff competition with Earl Johnson who lived closer to the Newsoms than Jason. Earl was close enough to walk about three miles to call on Sarah. Jason had to walk about six or seven miles unless he wanted to ride his mule or drive his family's buggy. The buggy was a classic and popular vehicle to go driving in to call on the girl. Every boy did not have access to a buggy and maybe able to take his girl for a buggy ride. Some families had not worked up to owning a buggy, too. The wagon was a *must* for the average post-slavery farming family, but the buggy could be non-essential if light trips were not usually made.

Jason was a reader who took every advantage of going to his one-room school nearer to him. He was a little older than Sarah. When she had turned "Sweet Fifteen," it was October 1894 and he was 19, having been born in 1875. Earl was closer to Sarah's age, and was such a steady young fella (very much a little gentleman, too). Sarah liked him because he was such a good-looking boy to be seen with. They would sit on the front porch in the settee sometimes when the weather was hot. Earl always wanted to sit and hold hands. Sarah found herself thinking warm thoughts about Jason when she was holding hands with Earl. Secretly, she longed for Jason to ask to call on her more often. She wondered if he had another girl or two and, if so, did he think of Sarah while he called on one of them just as she thought often of him while she walked, sat, and talked with Earl. "Oh God, please make Jason put me first in his heart. I know he's smarter than I am with his arithmetic, English and physiology, and his ability to debate with the best of his comrades and opponents. He reads books from white people's houses. They like to see him read because even though he's so smart, he'll never be allowed to take any of their places in this world. So, God, please make him like me better than any of those other gals. And, God, I may be a few years younger, but I'd try so hard to make him a good wife. If you gave us babies from our loving one another, I'd try as hard as I could to be as good a ma as my ma is to my pa and me. God, I know Jason is not as good-looking as Earl, but I don't care because when he holds my hand and talk to me like I am as smart as he is, I feel like shouting for joy. Oh, God, I'll keep a clean, pretty little house for us. I'll make good plum pudding and cold biscuit pudding. I will cook good butter beans and everything. And while I wait for him, I'll keep trying to be ready for him. I won't hurt Earl's feelings either. Lots of girls would be his girl, if he'd just let them know. Thank you, God."

Sarah felt Earl's nice warm hand in hers, and there swept over her a wave of happiness and a little guilt. He had no idea where her thoughts had been the last few minutes. They had traveled all the way to heaven. God had taken them because she gave them up to him. Now, she was going to have to wait to see what God would do with her thoughts that had become a prayer. Pa always said he prayed for God to do what was best because we don't always have sense enough to know what is best. Ma, on the other hand, would say that the Good Lawd does not ever, ever do nothing wrong. Now, with all that in mind, Sarah could only smile at Earl. Just then Ma came to the door and offered them some molasses cookies and buttermilk which both ate with enjoyment. Good warm molasses cookies and buttermilk that was cooled to drink by letting the covered pail down into the cistern.

Jason had been going over to see another girl who lived nearer to him (not often, but occasionally). It had started with a meeting at an ice cream supper on a Saturday night. Later she turned up at the church which he attended, and he had walked her home. He had seen Sarah earlier at her school program, which was held at the Baptist Church near her school. He had been very positively impressed with the reciting of Nathaniel Hawthorne's work and Paul Lawrence Dunbar's work by this young colored girl, Sarah Newsom, who demonstrated that she could read, and she could remember, *and* she could recite. Jason had inquired about this girl with such talent. Also, she was wearing a very pretty dress that looked as though it had been sto'-bought, not home-made like the other girls were wearing. Instead of braids on her head, she wore her thick black hair pulled loosely up to the top of her head and rolled into a loose bun right in the center of the top. All of this indicated that she was an unusual girl with unusual talents. He wanted to know more about this young girl who reminded him of an African princess. He was told that she was the best reader and speller in her school. Also, she could sew like a seamstress and do beautiful needlework, which made her the most envied girl at the colored school. He wanted to make her acquaintance, but obviously she was younger than he. What in the world would her pa and ma think that he was up to for coming after her? Nevertheless, he found out exactly where she lived in the valley.

Jason made a decision about how he might meet this girl. He went to her teacher and congratulated her for the really good job she had done preparing such a meaningful program that showed the talents of school children. He mentioned in particular Sarah Newsom. At that name, Miss Flowers' face lighted up. She volunteered, "Oh, there's a really special girl, an only child, not one bit spoiled, but very loved and knows how to love back, good manners, and so much more." He wondered what more could she have. He had not thought of the dress, which did not look like it was home-made in the least. Miss Flowers continued, "That girl can really sew and make beautiful knitted gloves, quilts, and the list goes on."

Jason said, "I'd sho' like to talk with her at home if you think her folks wouldn't mind." She answered that they would be pleased to meet the young man who led the Plum Creek Valley debate team. He sort of was taken aback because the teacher had not disclosed the fact that she knew this about him. He guessed the teacher wanted to see if he was for real about talking with this girl at home.

The other girl who had somewhat pursued Jason was not yet aware of her competition, Sarah Newsom. Jason, after meeting her and her parents, was almost consumed with thinking about her. He thought that he might be considered too old for her, but that was not the truth of the matter. Mattie and Lawrence really felt that this young man was real stable, smart in books, and smart about working. They thought that they could trust him to care for their little gal if he and she really liked each other.

Soon it became obvious that Sarah was liking Jason, and the same was true for him. Jason was mature just enough to be careful about rushing the courting of this nice smart girl. She was always glad in her heart when he wanted to come a courting, but Ma told her not to act too anxious because that could scare a man to death. He might start running and you could never, never "catch him."

Sarah was not to act so anxious, and she tried to keep that advice of her ma in her heart because it sho' 'nuf *was not* sinking into her head very deeply. When they walked behind her ma and pa as she and Jason held hands or when they sat on the porch settee and talked holding hands, Sarah's heart was beating warmly. She wanted Jason to kiss her on her lips. She knew he wanted to do the same thing, for whenever he got the chance he put his arm around her and squeezed her against him. She almost stopped wondering about him with

19

other girls. She was sure he was now spending his free time with her. Both of them were plenty busy. He did farm work just as she did. Only he had more man work to do in the fields, woods and barn than she. So she did more work in the house, yard and garden than she did in woods and fields.

Catherine was "taking company," too, and she had about three fellas who admired her. One of the fellas she had met in town one Saturday. She needed to find out more about him because her ma had told her to be careful about letting new boys court her if she knowed nothing much about them. One gal on Pine Hill met a handsome fella from Tall Point. She was letting him come a courting her and found out he had a wife and two babies (twin girls). He was sneaking off a-courting full time. His wife and babies were getting neglected while he dressed up and came to town on Saturdays. This turned into one big ugly mess. It was a lesson for the other single gals. Now all the mamas and papas keep sharp eyes and big ears for sneaky young rascals who might try to fool young gals.

Catherine had an older sister who was married to a ne'er-do-well man. They had three children (a beautiful girl baby and two boys almost old enough to go to school). When Catherine watched her sister struggling in a marriage that seemed to her to be more than Catherine would endure, she became determined to not make a great big mistake like that. Then she wondered to herself how would she be sure. Elizabeth must have thought that she knew, and just look what a mess she made. She has to get up early and hoe cotton until it's time to nurse the baby. Then she has to work hard until it's time to go back to the house and cook the noon meal and nurse the baby again and wash the dishes. Then back to work the field again until it's nursing time again and more hoeing cotton until it's time to go cook supper. While supper is cooking, she gets a quick chance to make up the beds for sleeping. She didn't have time to do this before she went to the field. She would run out to milk the cow and then put the supper on the table. Her husband never could or did help enough. He seemed to be a "good-for- nothing-setter-downer-before-all-the-work-is-done." He was what real folks called just plain "no good." Mattie would have said, "He thought God made way for all the seats in Plum Creek Valley for his behind to set down on." Sarah's ma called a spade a spade. She was known for her straight talk. Yet she loved everybody and everybody loved her because she was honest and truthful and good.

Elizabeth worked too hard all week long, and on Saturday the washing and ironing were waiting to be done. Bill, her husband, was very little help on the weekend also. If Elizabeth's family did not give a hand, things would be almost unbearable for her. Catherine wondered why her sister put up with so much of Bill's selfishness. She did not understand this part of the husband and wife thing. If it had not been for Elizabeth's widowed half-sick aunt helping her out, what would have happened? She had watched her ma and pa help each other with the work. When Ma was cooking, washing, scrubbing the floor, and such, Pa was feeding the stock, shucking ears of corn, shelling dry beans, gathering watermelons and such. Yet this husband of her sister didn't seem to know how to do anything after he left the field except make another baby for her sister to work some more for. The three kids were precious and lovable, but their daddy seemed to think his job was over when Elizabeth got "In the family way" again. This is not right.

Catherine had to look hard and long at the fella who wanted to marry her. She could can peaches, green beans, scrub the kitchen, and pick the cotton right at home for a long while more. Of course, one of the fellas who wanted to be her fella was the fifth son of a carpenter. He seemed to be a worthy young man. He could read, he could figure, and he did help his daddy with building houses, barns, cotton houses, smoke houses, etc. His name was David Smith. When David was not doing carpenter work, he did farm work like most of the colored boys in the late 1800s. David was able to keep Catherine more interested than the other fellas. When it was too cold to sit in the front porch settee, they would sit in the "front room." It was a sort of sitting room and bedroom combined. It was the largest room in most colored folks' houses and often had a fireplace instead of the heater. Fireplace made this room bright and cheerful all winter. Usually this room belonged to Ma and Pa. That was not a problem for the girl "taking company" and her beau because when bedtime came, the beau should have already started on his way home anyway.

Annie McFadden got married without there having to be a shotgun wedding. In fact, Annie was barely "showing." No one could have said for sure that she was "in the family way." She married in the little church house where she had gone to Sunday school. Sarah and Catherine were glad to go there to support Annie. Some gals were not allowed to attend the marriage because their elders felt it wasn't proper since Annie had not been a proper girl. They did not say that the groom had not been proper. Sarah's ma, Mattie, believed that Annie had been humiliated enough for her mistake; therefore, she asked Sarah to give Annie "something old, or something new something borrowed, or something blue," respecting the Victorian rhyme for a bride. Catherine was going to do the same. Sarah gave an old, but beautiful handkerchief. Catherine allowed her to borrow the little blue Sunday handbag that she carried when she had on her Sunday best dress. Annie looked real pretty. Sarah, Catherine and their mamas hugged Annie to wish her a happy life. The two papas shook hands with the groom and wished him happiness. Everyone was happy.

The right thing had been done, and the grown folks said God would bless the marriage. Mattie, always the one to speak her mind on what she felt was right, said, "I'm glad we went to see the marriage. Those folks who thought they gals too good to go or would be contaminated if they did go, better be awful careful. Yeah, awful careful, 'cause God sho' don' like ugly. He sho' don' like ugly a'tall! With that said, Mattie tucked her arm through Lawrence's and they walked across the road to get in the wagon to go home. They felt real good 'bout what they did today. Lawrence knowed that tonight Mattie was gonna let him hold her very close. Yeah, *very* close.

Mrs. Kelly, whose family's washing had been picked up on Monday morning for years, had not felt very well for a long time. Her oldest daughter, Miriam, the girl who had insisted on Lawrence stopping to eat breakfast, had taken her mother's place in the home. Since Miriam was more friendly and not so careful with Lawrence, he watched his steps because she was still a white girl who had brothers and a daddy. He did not want to become too relaxed and start shuffling, grinning and forgetting his colored man's place. On Monday as Lawrence knocked on the back door, Miriam was a very long time answering. So, he started calling out "Miss Miriam, Miss Miriam," and knocking again and again. Finally, Mr. Kelly came to the back porch and said that the doctor was with the family because Mrs. Kelly had just died. Lawrence was shocked and sorry at the news, for he had no idea that Mrs. Kelly's illness was so serious. He guessed he'd never allowed himself to think that far about this. Now, he found himself stammering for just the right words to say to this good

23

man who had just lost his wife. He did his best to think quickly of a few words that made sense. When he'd uttered those words, he swore to himself that they hadn't made much sense at all. He'd done his best; still he wondered if Mr. Kelly felt any better. Finally, after what seemed like a long time he said, "Let us know what else we can do. I'll take the clothes now and get them back tomorrow."

As Lawrence drove back out home, he found himself tapping old Buck lightly with the whip. He felt the need to go home in a hurry. The mule did not know why it was getting this extra message to go faster, faster. Lawrence was thinking what in the world would he and Sarah do if the "Good Lawd" would send the Death Angel after his Mattie. He couldn't stand to think about this, and he turned his thoughts toward creek and fishing. He found that it didn't help much this time. Lawrence had always enjoyed fishing. That was one of the things he looked forward to every year when crops were "laid-by." The whole family could sometimes go together. Mattie would put some cold biscuits, molasses and butter, tea cakes, peaches, tomatoes and a jug of water in the old cardboard box lined with an old clean bed sheet.

When the family went fishing like that, Sarah knew that she could ask Jason to go if she let him know in time. Her best friend, Catherine, could usually come along and was allowed to bring her fella, too. When the grown folks had other folks' chilluns with them, they felt just the same as if all were their chilluns. They made them all behave themselves and fish. There was one thing to be said for Sarah's fella, Jason Solley: he was very smart in books, and was such a mannerable boy. Because he was so mannerable and had such a good report, the Newsoms allowed something unusual, in their way of thinking. Jason could now take Sarah for a short buggy ride on a Sunday afternoon. There was a limit on the length of time they could be out and where they could go. They knew not to spoil that.

Jason learned to hold the horse's reins with one hand so that he could hold Sarah's hand that was next to him with the other. He knew better than to do that for more than a few minutes at a time; that was because he didn't want anyone to notice the careless driving and go tattling back to Mr. Newsom. He wanted to take no chances on losing this one great pleasure on a Sunday afternoon. Some Sundays they would stop by the Sanctified Church to listen to the people dance, sing, shout and clap, clap their hands. They belonged to the same denomination church, but it was not the Sanctified Church. So they found themselves sitting and listening. Sometimes they clapped their hands, too.

Lawrence was almost home when he realized just how much Mrs. Kelly's dying had shaken him up. What would Mr. Kelly do without his wife and a mother for their children? As soon as Mattie met him and the washings, she just knowed something bad was wrong. He started to tell her about Mrs. Kelly's dying. She stopped him with "Oh, Lawd, have mercy! Oh, Lawd, have mercy! I dreamt last night that I saw Miss Kelly flying, flying right through some pretty white clouds. I wondered what in the world she doing that fuh. I didn't see her come back down. Then I woke straight up and set up in the bed! It seemed so real that I looked over at you sleeping and that's when I knowed that I had dreamt it. Now, my dream don' come true. Miss Kelly have gon' behind those white clouds to the good Lawd in heben. I gots to hurry and finish these clothes. Then I gots to cook some chicken, greens, cornbread, and a good great big plum cobbler to carry them when the clothes are washed and ironed." With all that said,

Mattie got busy. It was just like her to wonder first what she should do and then to get on real busy doing it. She never felt like messing around when there was so much to be done. She'd just thank the Good Lawd that she never had been sick much, and that was a good reason not to mess around when somebody else needed help. Oh, no, she never doubted that. She was glad she didn't mind helping out people who needed her help. It was just the right thing to do. That's all there was to it.

While Mattie was doing the Kellys' washing, she found herself rubbing the clothes a little harder than before on the rub board. She was thinking about the Kellys, and she was thankful to whoever the man was who thought up to make a rub board. Just suppose she had to rub all of the clothes every week on her two hands. She thanked the Good Lawd for the rub board maker. By now he may be up behind the white clouds, too. She could still thank the Good Lawd for him because she could never turn out all of the washings this fast on her hands. Yeah, it would be much harder.

Then Mattie started thinking about the Kellys' food as she hung the sheets out on the clothesline. The sugar barrel was sho' gittin' low last time she filled from it. There had to be enough to sweetin that big plum pudding and maybe some teacakes, maybe. Yeah, had to be. She hurried all the more as her mind got so full of running 'round and 'round.

It was said by some of the white folks in town that Mrs. Kelly had died 'cause she got "change of life" problems. The doctor couldn't stop her monthly period from keeping on goin' and goin', Mattie explained to Sarah. She said, "Miss Kelly just plain bled to death. That's what she did!" So the Newsoms kept on washing and ironing for the Kellys. The extra money always came in real handy. Sarah could do it all by herself if she had to. If she kept on being smart and got herself a smart fella to love and cherish her, chances were good that she would just be washing only her own family's clothes in the future. She was looking forward to that.

Mattie thought to herself, "Yeah, my gal's gonna have a different life than her ma when it comes to doing white folks' work. If she married Jason, she just might not have to work other folks work (just her own family's work). Yeah."

Jason and Sarah

Jason Solley had smart brothers and sisters, too. One of his older brothers taught school. He could do this for colored children because he was so smart in books. He knew much more than the other boys or girls in and around Plum Creek Valley. Word was out he knew arithmetic and history better than any of the other chilluns, young or old. Some said he could conjugate verbs better than his teacher could when he was a school boy, and he could get the right answer to most all of the arithmetic problems even when nobody else could. He had been the first one in his class to learn the multiplication tables, and on and on.

One of Jason's sisters got a chance to attend Philander Smith College in Little Rock, Arkansas, for a while. It had been in existence since 1868 and it was a colored college. Jason was the baby of his family, and he hoped that he could one day attend Howard University in Washington, D.C. It had been established in 1867 about eight years before he was born, and he felt proud because it was a colored school, too. Jason's father died very suddenly, and school dreams faded for Jason. He didn't give up on reading, writing and figuring. He was just as smart as his teacher, many school children said. In fact, some said Mr. Dixon was actually very jealous of him at school. It was the school children who told their ma and pa what they noticed at school about that.

Jason became distinguished for his skill and power as a public speaker. His ability as an orator and a debater brought much respect for him. Sarah had always invited Lawrence and Mattie as well. They went to different churches, halls and schools on Friday or Saturday nights sometimes to hear him. Once in a while on Sunday afternoons he spoke. He was so glad to have his girl, Sarah, sit and cheer him on. When the programs were over, Sarah and Jason would find each other to walk hand in hand to the road home. Sometimes they walked to her house. Other times they rode, depending on how far it was. Then Jason had to go on to his home (much farther away).

These were good times (happy times for Sarah and Jason). They were both looking forward to more times together. Jason's mother could sometimes attend the programs and sometimes his sister, Ella, the oldest. Ella was almost a nurse, and a very good midwife, people said. She was called to more white ladies' bedrooms than any other midwife or doctor around Plum Creek Valley. They said she was good at her job of bringing babies out to the daylight. When she lightly spanked the white or colored baby until it cried, everybody was satisfied. Women died in childbirth more often than they did in later times, but most people thought if the life of the mother could be saved, Ella would do it. It was said about her that she was very quick to decide when she should send for the doctor. Yes, Jason's sister Ella had a good mid-wife reputation.

Sarah and Jason talked about things like Jason's saving his money. He was called on to do various jobs for white people. Not many colored boys were given the same chances, to work for white people as Jason. They could talk with Jason like he was a white boy, too, but Jason always remembered that they knew he was a colored boy, and he knew he was colored boy who was now becoming a man. He had a girl who could do just about anything. She had a wooden chest chocked full of pretty quilts that she had made. She could spell better than he could. One day he knew that she would be his wife. Then he could hold her as close as he wanted to when he wanted to. She would have his babies.

Sarah complained to Jason that she had never been a good cook even though she'd had so many chances to learn. He knew how to comfort her by letting her see how much he appreciated all of her other fine qualities.

In the meantime, Jason was his own boss in this community. White men reached out to this colored boy who read everything they passed on to him, and yet knew how to keep in his place by saying "Yessuh, Mr. Lewis; Yessuh, Mr. Clark; and Nosuh, Mr. Lewis; and Nosuh, Mr. Clark." Sometimes a white man or two would quietly come in where Jason was orating and sit down to listen. When the program was over, they would shake his hand and quickly leave for home. They thought that this colored boy was a very fine one. They hoped for him a house and field of his own for a good wife and children. They still gave him books.

It was still not far enough away from the American Civil War's end to let many colored men feel too satisfied about their present day place in the United States of America. This was a great big truth in the Deep South where the Newsoms lived. They wanted not only to be free from servitude, but find an honest way to a means for attaining their dreams. Most dreamed of a more satisfactory way of life for their children and for their children's children. All wanted the American way of life.

New Beginning

More than three years had passed since Sarah's "Sweet Fifteen" birthday celebration. Even though she and Jason knew in their hearts that they would some day soon get married, he had not gotten on his knees to ask her. Neither had he asked Lawrence and Mattie for her hand in marriage. While he longed for his Sarah and she longed for him, both knew that the time must be just right. One day as they sat on her front porch in the swing, he suddenly got up from his side of the swing and kneeled right before her, and without any hesitation asked for her hand in marriage. Before she could reply, Jason caught both her little hard-working hands in his huge hands and kissed them passionately. He hadn't known that he was going to do it just this way. With tears streaming down her face, she said, "Oh, my Jason, my Jason Solley, yes, I want to be your wife. This is a day I have waited for."

He answered her with something she had almost forgotten that she did. "I knew the first time I saw you do that beautiful curtsy after you had finished reciting some works of Paul Lawrence Dunbar and Nathaniel Hawthorne that I would someday be on my knees in front of you asking you to marry me. You looked just like an African princess. Now you will be my African princess, my very own. They stood together to go inside the house. Now, he would ask her pa and her ma.

He felt pretty good about how they would respond because he'd tried to always to be and act like a decent fella. His ma and pa taught him and his brothers to treat *their girls* just as good as they wanted other boys to treat *their own sisters*.

Mattie looked up from her embroidering and smiled. She could feel in her heart what this visit meant. So she touched Lawrence, who was trying to solve a maze in the weekly paper that came in the clothes basket from town. The young man faced the older man. He looked straight into the eyes of him, and without any stuttering or stammering at all, just said what he had left the porch to say, "I would be honored if I could marry your daughter, Sarah. I would love her always. Please say yes." The older man looked first at his wife, and then at Sarah, who was looking as happy as he'd ever seen her before, happier, in fact. Then smiling, he reached out his hand to the younger man and gave him and Sarah their blessings.

Mattie said it was time for a little early supper. So she asked Lawrence to get a chicken out of the "cleaning-out" coop in the backyard. This coop was keeping the chickens that needed to be cooked right away. No picking up a chicken right off the yard and cooking it that same day in Mattie's kitchen. Two or three are to be always fed good stuff until they were cleaned out enough to eat. Lawrence did wring the chicken's neck and skinned it (no time to heat water to scald the chicken and pick the feathers). No time today for that. Lawrence cut up the chicken while Mattie prepared some rice and canned green beans. She opened a jar of blackberries and made a "quickie" drop dumpling pie while the chicken was smothering in a covered frying pan.

Soon Mattie asked Lawrence to bring up a jug of cool buttermilk that was hanging down in the cistern. Rain had been good this year, and the cistern kept plenty of cool rainwater. The family would use an extra rope to let down the covered bucket of milk to cool. Mattie and Lawrence looked at each other and smiled. Their baby was going to marry that nice boy, Jason. With that, they set the table and called the newly engaged couple to it. This was not a time for Sarah to do anything except sit down with her fella and eat. The food must be blessed now.

Lawrence took his place at the head of the table. Mattie took her place at the foot. Jason and Sarah faced each other, one on each side of the table. The older couple and newly engaged couple could now look each other right in the face. It seemed that everything was cooked just right, or was it everybody's imagination? If so, imagination could come in mighty handy. The family and the soon-to-be family felt like no afternoon could be better. "The Good Lawd sho' is smiling down on us. He sho' 'nuf is," Mattie said to herself.

Sarah felt that not another gal in the country could be more satisfied than she was right now. She is going to marry her all-time favorite fella. Sarah was "going on" 19 years old. Her hope chest was becoming pretty full of quilts, sheets and embroidered pillowcases, under skirts, bloomers and flour sack drawers. What girl could be fixing to get married if she didn't get ready with these things? Most of them started to quietly get their hope chest filled long before they were engaged to be married. The older women thought, "Most ever' gal is going to git herself a husband, and ain't no needs her fooling 'round to not be ready when the time do come." Therefore, the young gal was taught to piece pretty quilt tops out of scraps of cloth left from dresses, shirts and pants. They also used scraps left from cutting down and making over secondhand clothes given to them by white people. Some people called these clothes hand-me-downs. No matter what they decided to call them, smart colored women could find some good use for them during these years between 1865 and 1935 especially. Seventy years and still hand-me-downs were still live and kicking.

Sarah's quilt tops that she had been piecing for a few years were now to come out of the chest and made into quilts. This meant there would be a "quilting bee" held at the Newsom household. For the quilting bee the quilting frames were lowered down from the ceiling with pulleys, so that the women could put the cotton batting (flattened-out cotton) between the pieced quilt top and the lining and then hand-stitch together. The linings usually were made with sewn-together bleached flour sacks or any other sacking material. This was to keep from having to use up scarce money for a quilt lining. Since these quilts had greatly varied patterns in the tops, most were quite beautiful. Every gal in Plum Creek Valley wanted to be known for her quilt-making skills. These quilts made warm cover, and they served as bedspreads also.

Mattie did not want to frighten her very happy child; however, she thought it fair to tell her that every day of her upcoming marriage would not be easy. Sometimes she would shed a tear. Sometimes she would wonder what next, but always she would have to keep on keeping on because Jason loves her, she loves him, and most and best of all, the Good Lawd loves both of them. Also, when they have chillun, the Good Lawd would love them and the chillun.

Sarah did love her ma a whole lot because of so many things, for trying to shield her, trying to prepare her, trying to lift her up, if she thought Sarah needed it. She would very often wish that she could expect to be as good a ma as her ma. Then she'd think that she was almost asking too much.

Not many people were up to her ma. She was also a steady, strong, loving wife to her pa. She heard her ma say more than one time how she guess she would have been "an old maid" if Lawrence had not come into her life. Ma thought herself to be a hard-to-please gal. She changed this when Lawrence became her best beau. Here was a man Mattie could put her trust in. Here was a man she could love at last. Any doubts or fears she would put to rest now because she would love him forever.

Mattie knowed she had to tell Sarah the one thing that could wait no longer. First, she had to talk it over with Lawrence. Some surprises are easy to hear. Some surprises hurt to hear. Some surprises kill to hear. They had agreed that it was now the time to tell Sarah that she had a half-sister who is two years younger than Sarah. She does not live in Plum Creek Valley. She does not even live in the state. It had happened years ago when Lawrence had taken a temporary job on a white man's farm many miles from his own valley. While he worked there, he stayed for six days in the men's servant house, a few yards away from the main house yard. The young colored woman who did the housekeeping stayed in a one- room servant house in the main house back yard. That was when it happened. Mattie had no idea when Lawrence returned to her and Sarah after the six days' good-paying job, that anything bad had happened. She was so happy to see him, and he seemed equally as happy to see her and Sarah.

This was a surprise not easy to hear. It hurt so bad to hear, and it almost did kill her to hear. Mattie had felt like she was just dying when Lawrence was forced to tell her that truth. She just knew that she would soon wake up from this terrible nightmare, and Lawrence would be sleeping 'side her. He would not have betrayed her. This was the man she loved above any other fella. This was the man she trusted. This was the man that made her know she didn't wanna be "an old maid" as she had sometimes thought. She had never cared this much about any fella. Mattie knowed she was just going to die. Lawrence begged, cried, patted and explained. Yet she knowed that she would die! She wouldn't die even if she could! She had her baby! She still had her Lawrence! He was not the Good Lawd. He was just a man. He was still her man who had made the big mistake of killing her. He did not bury her, though. So, she forgave him after he begged so pitiful like. Mattie knowed when she made up her mind that it was made up. That's the way she was. Lawrence was hers now and forever, and he knowed that he was fully forgiven and him and Mattie were forever.

The True Story Continues

This was the true story that their Sarah had to hear. Sarah had to hear it. She had to know that a good life has its low places, which can make the high places seem higher.

One day there will be a meeting between Sarah and her half- sister, between her daddy and her half-sister and Mattie. This is what needs to be. This will be! Mattie will see to this! Years had gone by before Lawrence heard about his young daughter. Even then, he didn't know that this was true. He knowed full well that it could be true before his second daughter showed up at their front gate. He saw himself all over again just like looking into a giant looking glass. Lawrence was so glad that he had trusted his wife with the truth of his past weakness. He had told this to himself again and again.

Pearl did not write a letter to the pa she had never seen before, but she was able to find him by the pieces of information her ma had given her. Her ma had married, and Pearl had a stepdaddy who had kept her just like she was his own blood ever since he and her ma got married while Pearl was very little. Now, she was almost 17 years old, and her ma had died a few months before.

Mattie had decided that if this time ever did come 'round, the child would be welcomed in their house. Mattie was true to her own mind. Sarah and Pearl liked each other quickly.

Lawrence and Pearl had a few awkward minutes until Mattie and her wisdom stepped in. She hugged Pearl real tight and said, "Well, we all just one big family now! You hungry, Pearl? I'm 'bout to starve to death!" Without another minute passing up, Mattie started setting the table for the food was already cooked. Lawrence and Pearl started to talk lively. They enjoyed their meal a whole lot.

Pearl stayed the night and would ride to town to get the train home the next day. They all rode in the wagon to the train station. They decided that this would happen again in the future. When they parted, Sarah was the first to hug her new sister. Then Lawrence and Mattie followed. This felt like a new piece of a pretty quilt for the Newsoms. They were all ready to keep in touch by writing some letters. Yes, they would keep the mail carrier a little more busy. Sarah, Lawrence and Mattie paid Pearl's full fare.

As Pearl waved good bye when the little train was moving down the railroad tracks, she thought about having another pa and a new ma and a big sister. She would write them a letter after she got home. She would think about all of them. Maybe next time she would get to see her new sister's fella. Sarah told her all about him last night while they were talking and talking.

Jason and Sarah had set their wedding date for October 25th, Sarah's 19th birthday. When they were trying to pick a date, it was Jason who thought of her birthday. Then he said laughing, "Now, I'll never be able to forget your birthday." She answered also laughing, "Well, you better not if you know what is good for you, Mr. Jason Solley!" Then they chuckled together like two little kids. They were kids at heart right now.

While Sarah had been getting quilts and other house things sewn and ready, Jason and his brothers and friends had been getting their home ready for the big day. Sarah had never had her picture made (not once yet, but that was not unusual in the year 1898, especially for a colored girl). But this was a very special occasion. Mattie and Lawrence knew that this picture had to be made for keeps. Their Sarah could look at it for many years to come. Even though Sarah was so much waiting for this special day, she had many unanswered questions about this special night. Ma was happy and satisfied about the wedding day, but not one word was said about the wedding night. Sarah thought back to that day some years ago when she had been hoeing corn in the field with Pa. Something was happening high between her legs that Ma had not told her about. She was remembering that Ma had thought it was not time to talk about it yet. Sarah guessed this was just the same way. Then she'd find out that night when she pulled off her clothes and put her long, lacy cotton nightgown on. Ma had made sho' that Sarah's nightgowns were trimmed with lace.

There was one thing for sure, Sarah was thinking that by night she would be the wife of Mr. Solley. Oh, she had so much to look forward to. In her Sunday School she learned that the Good God of everything would bless her and Jason because they were now one.

Jason had not lost time (not in a long time), because he wanted to have a house for him and Sarah to live in. They would not have to live with Sarah's parents at the beginning of their marriage like some of the people he had known or heard about. Therefore, for a long time Jason had spent his spare time getting the place that would be their home in order. It was located nearer to the white folks' community than it was to the colored folks. It just turned out that this was the house that Mr. Dixon, who had been one of Jason's teachers, directed him to; and Rev. Clark whose clothes had been

39

washed so nice and whose white shirts had been starched and ironed so pretty by Sarah and her ma for so long, used his influence for Jason. This place was just right, even though on Sundays they would go a little farther to church and the schoolhouse would be a little farther away. These things would be a small price to pay for having a place of their own so soon after Jason and Sarah married.

Jason wanted fruit trees. Peaches and pears grew well in this part of the South. They must have some fig trees, too. The Bible spoke of fig trees. So Jason planted rows and rows of peach trees in a spot outside of the west fence (their peach orchard). He planted different kinds of peach trees. Some would start to ripen early and some a little later, and still some a little later. So they would have fresh peaches all through the summer. There were two fig trees, one on each side of the back yard. There were two pear trees in one corner of the huge garden in the back of the house. These trees had to grow for a while before they started to bear fruit. That was all right, Jason and Sarah thought. Anything worthwhile was worth waiting a while for. They had both heard these words all of their lives. Now they would have to believe them.

Their house had one fireplace and one heater, besides the cook stove. Between the two of them, Jason and Sarah was just about ready to start housekeeping. They would welcome not only the well-wishing words, but they would also welcome any marriage gifts. The Clarks and the Kellys seemed to remember the years of clean clothes with some quite nice used household things like black iron pots, teakettles, pans, plates, knives, forks and spoons. Jason's sister Ella, who did mid-wifing for whites as well as colored folks, was given some things for her baby brother Jason and his wife Sarah. They had heard good things about this one colored smart boy and his girl who could sew and do such pretty needle work, and had been the best speller in her school. Yes, they wanted to help Ella's brother.

Sarah's Wedding

    On the day of the wedding, Sarah's best friend, Catherine Kelly, came over to help Sarah look her prettiest in an outfit that was fashionable. Sarah had made it. It was a blue full-length, very wide skirt, fitting really tight at Sarah's tiny waist, and the bodice was white with long puff sleeves. The dress was belted with a black patent leather belt to match Sarah's shoes. Sarah wore her thick black hair pulled loosely up the top of her head and rolled into a loose bun right in the center of the very top. This was exactly the way she was wearing it when Jason had first seen her reciting at the school program. Yes, exactly.
    Catherine was really happy for her best friend, and she would be looking forward to the same wonderful favor in exactly two months. Yes, Catherine was engaged to her best beau of all times, and they would be married on Christmas Day. Oh, how God was smiling on these two friends, Catherine smiled to herself again.
    Jason and Sarah had gone to their very own house to spend their wedding night. This was not always done with colored newly weds. Many of them had to spend that night in the bride's ma's and pa's house. Everything was ready. Pretty coverlets on the bed, and a nice washstand with bowl, pitcher, hand towels and soap stood against the wall (all but coverlets were gifts).

The young couple remembered what they had been taught, and before they settled in for the night, they knelt by their double bed with the solid oak wood tall headboard and a shorter footboard. They said their prayers. Jason prayed aloud. Yet Sarah prayed with him to God in her heart. They thanked God for his love for them and then for their love for each other to continue to get stronger. Jason asked God to help them to never forget him throughout their life together. They said their Amens and blew out the coal oil lamp, which Rev. Clark had bought for them. This item was not second-hand. The Clarks were remembering all the pretty washes this little colored gal had helped her ma do for them. The wash was never less than satisfactory in all these years. This Sarah Newsom was now 19.

Mattie had told her little gal when they were gittin' ready for the wedding that she would not have to help anymore, and that she had done good. Now she would do only her own household's washing and ironing. Never again did Sarah "take in" washings. Mattie had said her gal's life was gonna be easier than hers, and she meant to help start this herself right here. There was no argument with Jason about this. He had a big garden plot and a pretty big flower-growing space in the front yard, and the fruit trees, and then babies would come. All of this would keep Sarah as busy as she needed to be. Jason did not want Sarah ever guiding a big middle buster plow down farm rows. He believed that if he tried hard enough, the Good Lawd would hear his prayer about this, and it won't ever happen. No, no!

From this time on, the young couple started living normally. Sarah took care of inside the house and outside the house. There was one thing that Sarah intended to have just like her ma always had, and that was a chicken coop to "clean out" the chicken to eat right away. No eating chickens that had run free all over the place and had eaten anything they pleased. Her ma had drilled that into her. She had seen Ma take some boards, a handsaw, nails and hammer to make a chicken coop to look like a little house. Ma said the little roof needed to be slanted and not flat so that the rain could run off like people's houses. Then after the two or three chickens were corn-fed, they were then fit to eat. Sarah had heard this so much. Now she believed it, and that's just what she did.

Oh, yes, Sarah was enjoying all parts of this new life. Jason seemed to think her cooking was fine. She knew it wasn't as good as Ma's, but maybe when she stared to see her babies growing up, they would believe her cooking was good just like she did her ma's cooking.

Ma's patching clothes on the knees, elbows and anywhere else to save a piece to wear some more was something that Sarah had learned to do almost like Ma. She had been told that she could take old newspaper and a catalog from the mailbox, look at a dress, shirt or bloomers, then cut out a pattern and make it just like in the catalog. She was getting to like the way she could do it, too. Sarah smiled to herself. All was well with the Good Lawd's world, and they were in it.

Jason was busy with many things. Besides taking care of the fall harvesting, he continually prepares orating and debating materials on different subjects. He showed extraordinary interest in colored folks' welfare, both adults and children. The colored school's board elected Jason president because they felt he was the best man for this job. He had been accepted as a member of the Prince Hall Free Masonry, which was an organization for Negroes. In 1791, this organization headed by a Negro Methodist minister protested slavery. It was in this that many Negroes of prominence became members. In their church Jason was a leader. He was good, smart and fully able to do what was expected of him. White folks said he had integrity.

Sarah made a good mate for Jason. She became an Eastern Star, a women's lodge group affiliated with the men's Masonic Lodge. She worked as a Sunday School teacher and missionary study leader. She was doing as much as she could while she still could, for when their babies started increasing, Sarah's time would become less and less. God would not bless her to be a ma and then be happy for her to neglect the children he gave them. She would be real careful.

Their babies had started coming in 1900. They had married in 1898. Almost every two years or thereabout, another little Sarah and Jason Solley baby peeped its little Solley head around the corner. They remembered what the Bible had said about being fruitful and multiplying. It seemed they had not much choice in the matter unless they were going to stop loving each other. Anyway, they loved each other and all the babies too much to think of such a thing. Sarah was thankful that Jason's sister, Ella, the midwife, had always been able to take care of her. Sometimes a ma died in childbirth and that was a scary thought. The Good Lawd musta left Sarah here for something.

Lawrence and Mattie seriously considered what they should do now to make Pearl, the other daughter, become more of the daughter that blood said she was. Mattie, always straightforward and very fair, told her husband that it was time for them to make Pearl a real sister to Sarah and a real daughter to her and her real father, Lawrence. Mattie came right out and said, "This nice young gal didn't have a single thing to do with being in this family or in this world, for that matter. So, we gots to stop treating her like she did. We gots to send her a letter with her train fare in it asking her to come and visit us again. We needs to ask her to bring her two boys to visit. They needs to know their grandpa, and me, their other grandma, and Sarah, their aunt, and Uncle Jason, and their cousins. If some of us have to sleep on a pallet, that's sho' all right 'cause I gots plenty of clean quilts. Yeah!"

Lawrence agreed to all of this while thinking over and over what a lucky man he was to have such a wife with this big heart. No, no, not a mean little bit in this lady. She don' know what meanness is. He then went to his chewing tobacco can behind the bureau near the head of their bed to see how much he had saved up from the watermelons and sweet corn that he sold in town. Also, he had saved up something from potatoes. When Lawrence counted, he was sure he had enough for the train fares. Yeah, that would be enough to cover it. He started to get really excited.

Mattie had enough saved to buy some cloth for making clothes and for thread. She would make some cotton shirts and britches for the boys. She would make Pearl a skirt and puffed long-sleeve blouse. She would have to guess the sizes from the ages for the boys. Pearl was about her size. So she would measure for Pearl by her clothes. When they arrived, all would be ready. What a good surprise! How happy this thought made Mattie feel! They would get started on all of this tomorrow. Oh, oh, what a good time this would be. They told Sarah and Jason about the plan and, of course, they told the children. Everybody was looking now for "company coming" to visit in Plum Creek Valley. Yeah, company coming.

All was ready and the fares were in Pearl's hand. They could wait for the day for company to come. They would go to meet the train, and then they would all start the visiting. Sarah got a good glimpse of what having her own sister was like, and the cousins had a good time after they got over being jealous of one another about the attention Grandma Mattie was giving to the newly found cousins. Children are not a bit like grown folk. They get over things fast, and next thing they are laughing and skipping and riding down horsey-horsey bushes together.

Sarah cooked and Mattie cooked. The men and boys did the outside work. Everybody had a rollicking good time for about three days. Then it was over and they were all waving bye-bye.

The children learned that they all knew about picking cotton, picking green peas, and toting water to the field to give drinks to the older field workers. They all knew that as soon as they got old enough they would do the same things as the older ones. This was not saying though, that they had to like it. In fact, some of them had already been daydreaming about someday when they would not be working in that hot sun all day long. They were thinking that they would find another way.

Lawrence

It had been raining for three days, and Plum Creek was rising, rising. The rain came, but Lawrence was still planning and intending to get into town. In fact, there were a few supplies that they needed. Mattie knew they could wait for them. She tried to get Lawrence to wait until the rain stopped, but he was and had always been determined to go when he thought he should; that was how he did things (a very determined man). Mattie had to respect that.

Since Lawrence didn't mean to have enough things for the wagon and two mules, he took the buggy. A buggy sho' 'nuf did come in mighty handy around their place. As soon as Lawrence thought the rain had let up, he hitched up the mule and buggy, climbed happily into his seat, waved goodbye to Mattie, and off he went to town. He was thinking that since the rain was almost gone now, it would not take long to pick up his things and be on his way home again. That would be over.

As he neared Plum Creek, he could see that water had really been falling a whole lot. Then he thought that maybe the rain was about over and the creek would start to go down. He could look forward to gittin' a little fishing done when the creek settled down again. Seemed like he never could git to fish as much as he liked. Then he thought about how the

Good Lawd never can quite satisfy us human beings. We seem to always be wantin' sompn' different from what he gives us. We forgits he know better than us human beings. We always forgittin'.

After Lawrence had finished his buying in town, he noticed that the clouds were dark again, real heavy like. Now, if he really hurried he could git back home befo' there was too much more rain. He loaded his things into the buggy and struck out for the brisk ride home. The rain started again. It poured down like a big storm. Lawrence thought maybe he should pull over to some white folks' yard, but no, if he kept hurrying he could git cross the bridge befo' the water got any higher. So he really went faster, faster and faster. As he approached the bridge, the water had gotten even higher than before. It was a good thing he didn't stop to wait 'cause he might not been able to git home till next day, and that had never happened befo'. Mattie would be worried to death, and with that he tapped his old mule and they started cross the bridge, but something was goin' wrong. The bridge was swaying, swaying, and the mule was trying to swim. The buggy was on its way down Plum Creek. The old bridge musta played out. "Oh, Lawd, have mercy! Lawd, please, please have mercy on us," but Lawrence felt himself floating out of the buggy and all goin' downstream. Nobody was out there to help. Down, down, down, Lawrence went. The mule and the packages and the buggy all going away from Lawrence.

At home Mattie had been really worried for a long time. She was so worried about all of this new rain. She wondered if Lawrence stopped somewhere until the rain slowed up. It was night, and so long ago she should have heard or seen something of her Lawrence. She needed to git word to Sarah and her crew, but she also needed to stay as close to the house as possible so that she would be there when Lawrence came. Yeah, she better stay right here and wait for Lawrence! Oh Lawd! All night Mattie waited, and then she thought some of them good white people don' 'suaded Lawrence to wait 'til daylight to go back out home. It was still dark, but almost day again. She had stretched out on the bed to wait because she stayed wake all night. Then she must have dozed off for a minute or two. Somebody was beatin' and beatin' on her front door. She jumped up and ran to the door. There stood the county sheriff and one mo' man. They asked was I Mattie Newsom and I said, "Yesuh, I sho' is her! Where my Lawrence, suh? Suh, where my Lawrence?" Oh, now Mattie was gittin' the wuss feeling that she had ever had in all her born days.

The county sheriff felt so sorry to tell her. He took off his hat and said, "I am so sorry to bring you this really bad news. Your husband is dead. He drowned in Plum Creek yesterday. The water was too high and he washed away with the buggy, mule and all. I am so sorry. We found his body, and you can come claim it for burying him. I hated to bring you this sad news! We all knew what a good man Lawrence was."

Mattie finally found her voice again. She said to the sheriff, "Mr. Sheriff, would you please take me to my daughter's house so I can tell her 'bout her pa. She is just gonna die. I cain't stand to go by myself." And with that, for the very first time, Mattie broke down and really cried.

The officer had to forget for a moment that this woman who was born a slave girl and who married a slave boy was still a colored gal. He had to forget that this grieving, heartbroken woman was not white, and he thought more about this mission after it was finished. He even dreaded complying with the request that Mattie had just made. It was not because he didn't want to or didn't have time to; it was because his heart went out to both these women. It had really touched this white officer's heart.

Mattie, Sarah and Jason did what they were directed to do, and Lawrence was laid to rest the following day. It was really a very serious and sad thing, which just tore up Mattie's heart and did not seem natural that Lawrence was now in the ground. The casket was constructed of pine. The colored burials at that time were done almost immediately because many could not be embalmed. Funeral homes became available and popular a little later for many colored people. At the time of Lawrence's tragic death, next day and third day funerals were necessary because the bodies would start to decay. Summer burials had to be done faster than winter burials, of course.

This was a time for a new beginning for the Newsom and Solley houses. All of the grandchildren would miss their grandpa because he had taken them with him fishing and chopped grass with him. He had made them feel good when they were with him. Pearl did not get to attend her pa's burial. There was not enough time for her to receive a letter and then catch a train. By the time Pearl got the letter, her pa was already buried. Pearl wrote to stepmother Mattie and to sister Sarah, and they wrote letters to her. They promised to always write and visit whenever they could. They never forgot to do this because finding each other had been a blessing. All of them lived in the deep South. All were still struggling to overcome the bites and scars that slavery had left. Though the institution of that dark thing, slavery, was officially over, it would take a much longer time before any of them would see what they were dreaming of.

Many colored people were still struggling for better living conditions and better schools with longer terms. It took a whole lot of work to get better housing, and even after working, pay was not sufficient to allow for that. Education sorely needed to be improved. This was a fact that if attended to would lead to better paying jobs, and that would lead to many needed things for colored people. Mattie had always been thinking of how she wished she could do more to see to it that not only her grandchildren, but all other colored children would have a chance that she didn't have. She sho' didn't want them to have to be washers and ironers for other people, no matter how nice they were. She always had said these things to her Lawrence. He had wanted all of this as much as Mattie; he just didn't say as much as she did about it. They used to laugh together and say that she talked about everything good enough for both of them, and it was good that she was not doing bad talk.

The Solley Family Living

Sarah and Jason thought a whole lot about their children and what their futures might be like. Sarah had borne 14 children since they were married on Sarah's birthday, October 25, 1898, when she was exactly 19 years old. They had been blessed that none of these were stillborn and Sarah had lived through every birth. All of their children had been born in their right minds. However, they wanted more for their children than they had been able to have. Although Jason was born in 1875 and had done very well in school, he didn't get to go to school nearly as much as he had wanted to. He still dreamed of Howard University.

Sarah was much more fortunate than either of her parents had been. Even though she learned fast, there had not been nearly enough time spent in school. She was happy that her children were attending more. She enjoyed sharing her school experiences with them. She loved to tell them about the spelling bees, which she had much fun taking a very active part in. They were great incentives for her. She told them how hard she studied for this because she enjoyed being the last one standing. Her children loved listening as much as their mother loved telling this. They could see her becoming excited all over again. She told them how she learned to spell extra long words. Sarah had not heard the term phonetics, but she had a natural super-talent that she knew how to put to use when reading or writing.

Since Sarah was so aware of her own limited education, she constantly encouraged the children to read, write, do arithmetic and spell. As a result, they listened not only to her constant encouragement, but they eagerly watched their pa's speeches and his sharing of newspaper articles. Even though he was constantly using his talents, he always longed for more formal education.

All of Jason and Sarah's children were trained to some degree, either formally or informally, to make an honest livelihood. They never ceased to be amazed at their parents' love of learning and their love and total respect for each other. Their parents had been blessed to stay in love. They still would hold hands going to and from church or a school program. Jason made sure that he looked out for Sarah. She did the same for him. They never made a fuss about it, but they always did it. Neither of them ever seemed to tire of learning something new.

As their children went away to schools, marriages, jobs, etc., Sarah kept her writing skills honed by speeding letters to them. She tried to answer them soon. She didn't believe in letting letters remain unanswered for long. At first she did as she had learned to do in her school. She wrote her letters with pencil and ruled paper. Then she moved up to using a fountain pen. It took a little more time and care dipping the pen in her ink bottle, but Sarah felt good. Jason was already doing this. He was a frequent user of paper. She smiled about her Jason because he tried to be so sophisticated. She learned that word after she had stopped going to school. She smiled to herself again.

When her children asked her what she wanted for her birthday or for Christmas, she requested practical things like pen, ink, writing paper. Since she loved to embroidery, she might ask for that kind of thread, making sure she said the colors she needed.

When Sarah's children needed any kind of help that she could give, she got right to it (no slowing around). One of Sarah's boys was so eager to start to school before he was quite old enough, so she decided to teach him some of what she knew about first grade. There was no kindergarten in their school. So to stop Edward from crying every day to go to school with his older brothers and sisters, she kept him busy for part of the day learning his ABCs and counting to 100. Then he learned to spell a little, read a little, and became very, very proud of himself. He sometimes could hardly wait to show his pa and his sisters and brothers that he had been to school, too. Sarah would brag on Edward, and it made him more eager. The proudest person of all in this little drama was the man of the house, Jason. He was so proud of little Edward, but in his heart, he was most proud of his Sarah. He never ceased to be amazed by his wife, and she never got too busy for him. Of course, that was a mutual thing. He always included Sarah's needs in his thoughts and activities.

When Sarah was having their 14 babies, eight boys and six girls, he made sure that the six weeks' confinement period for a mother was strictly kept by Sarah. Some men might feel they needed their wife's work before that time, but Jason would never have considered it. He just wanted his Sarah to be completely well when she took over their new baby and housework. Jason would get up a little earlier every day for that six weeks required after a woman had a new baby. He did extra things before he went to his outside work. He returned to the house to do or help do the chores that still needed to be done. With 14 children coming into the Solley house over a span of about 25 years, Jason could, after a while, get plenty of help from the older children. Sarah had constantly trained them well. Jason did wash cotton diapers.

A great advantage of being a part of a big family was the process of passing on knowledge. The younger children kept learning from the older ones. So it was important to Sarah and Jason that they put their best foot forward. So much of what the older children knew and did seemed to get into the young Solleys without too much adieu. Everyone could see that when the older children did their schoolwork, the young ones were impressed more than they knew themselves.

Sarah shared her quilting, sewing and knitting time with the children whenever it was possible. She constantly rewarded them for learning efforts with tight hugs. They tried harder.

Lawrence, Sarah's pa, had always said, "Watch out for the company you keep." She thought of that so many times. There was that Joe Baker boy, so sneaky and sly. She did not trust him around their girls. Yet, she didn't want him with the boys his age either. He didn't have any manners, and he didn't like to go to church either. Those were two things that they believed in here at the Solley house. She had to find some way to help him, and she finally decided that instead of making him an outcast, she maybe should start trying to be his friend. In fact, she really did feel sorry for him. His ma was said to be very withdrawn. She believed he did not go places with his daddy like her boys. Yes, Sarah would become his friend, and she'd tell Jason about her new idea. Both of them would be his friends instead of being scared and hating him. This way was not helping anybody and especially Joe Baker. When she put her mind to something, she was like her own ma, she meant to do it.

Joe Baker was sometimes asked to come over and eat a Saturday or Sunday meal with them. Mattie had always told Sarah that a warm meal did do good things for people. Sarah knew this was true. She always tried to have that when her own crew came in from school or field or the woods. Yes, a warm greeting and a meal keeping warm on the cook stove. Since Sarah did not ever go to the field after she married, she could just stop everything else and get the food ready. She admitted to herself that she so much hated to stop in the middle of a job that she was trying to finish. Anybody around her could see this. Yet, she was just not going to say it out loud to *anybody,* and with this thought she smiled to herself. Jason had things which kept him busy enough to welcome mealtime from the barn, shucking corn, shelling dry corn from the cobs, picking peanuts off the dry vines, and farming stuff like this. Sometimes he sat by the fireplace reading or rereading some of the books, which he dearly loved. Every chance Jason got for free time he would read.

Sarah met him with her famous special smile when he came in from the barn or field. She would tell her children when they came from school to quickly take off their clothes and hang them up (no laying them around to clutter up their home). They did not do their night work and study their school lessons in their school clothes. School clothes were not changed daily. They were changed on Fridays. The Friday clothes were usually kept for Sunday. So they could not afford, at anytime, to eat in their clothes. Everybody hurried to sit at the table and eat the dried beans, peas, fruits or the greens, which would sometimes stay in the garden until the frost fell on them. When dinner was over, they hurried to do their work.

Filling the coal oil lamps was a careful and painstaking job. The oil could easily spill, which was both messy and costly. It had to be paid for in town just like sugar, salt and flour. Some things just could not be grown in the garden or in the field. One of the night jobs that could not be forgotten was cleaning the ashes from the heating stove and fireplace. The kitchen stove might have to be cleaned of ashes before making the new fire to cook the breakfast. Jason or the cook might do this. It was quicker and easier than the other ashes. None of the ashes were, however, just dumped out, but saved in a can or some buckets for future use. Ashes were kept in the outdoor toilets, or "outhouses" as they were often called, to pour in the toilet holes, to make lye solutions, or putting into the cuspidors or spittoons. Except for the sake of company, Sarah's family spat in the fireplace or the wood stove.

While quilting on the wooden quilting frames that hung from the ceiling to be rolled up at bedtime or when not in use, Sarah would sometimes delight her younger children with old, old stories. The children would gather happily around the fireplace to not miss a single word, and Sarah would not miss a single stitch as she quilted. She had always had a great passion for living, which was matched by Jason's joy of reading historical books, for writing speeches and learning mathematics. He depended on his mathematical skills to figure quite accurately the number of shingles to cover his barn, his sheds and the house they lived in. These kind of things he thoroughly did enjoy.

Jason would stop reading his history, physiology, and whatever else he was reading to talk about the great Booker T. Washington. He felt a real closeness and kinship to the man who had set out to help young colored youngsters to be somebody (somebody more than cotton pickers and sugar cane strippers and hackers). That was the aim of Jason; that was his dream. He was a man for sharing inspirational stories that really were not stories at all. When he told the story of Abraham Lincoln walking many miles to borrow a book to read by pine-knot light or maybe a lamp light, one child asked her pa, "Wasn't Abraham Lincoln a white boy, and what made *him* have to read by a pine-knot light? Seems like he wouldn't have to do things like poor colored chillun had to sometimes do. *We* even have lamps. Sometimes we almost run out of coal oil though."

Then Jason tried to answer his little thinking girl's thought-provoking question. He tried never to evade questions that his children asked him. If they were smart enough to think about it, then they were smart enough to understand the answer he would give them. Therefore, he always answered, as he understood the question. He said to his child, "All white people are not rich or *even* well-to-do just because they are white. Abraham Lincoln was a white boy who was smart and enjoyed reading and learning. That was one of the reasons he wanted to become the President of the United States of America. He wanted to keep his country in good shape and also make conditions much better for everybody. He was the reason that we are not still slaves, but my ma and pa were slave children before 1865."

Alexander Graham Bell had invented the telephone 1877 when Jason was only two years old. Jason had gotten married in 1898 when he was 23. At that time he wondered how long it would take for the telephone to be in common use. He was interested in it, not because he needed it for business or his farm work, but because it was to him a sign of progress. He and Sarah would like to feel that they were somehow progressing if they could have a telephone. Then he thought that this was just idle workings of their minds. So many things should come in their lives for their children's benefit before

Mr. Bell's talking device. Yes, the telephone would have to wait. If a colored family had an urgent message to get or to send, there was usually a nice white family close enough to receive or send it. One day that time came much quicker than any of the Solleys thought when Charley hollered loud from an accident with the ax while chopping wood. If it had not been for the white neighbor's telephone, the doctor said Charley would have bled to death. The bleeding was finally checked and just barely in time. So much good for telephones. Yes, they were a useful invention the Solleys could see. One day they would have one.

The Solley children worked hard, studied hard and went to school as much as time and school terms would permit. The boys sawed a lot of wood, ploughed many rows of corn, cotton, and other farming things. The girls did a lot of farm work, but also had learned how to do the housework as soon as Sarah thought they were old enough. Sarah felt very blessed to have six girls and eight boys. When they had relaxing time, there were no televisions or radios available to them. So they listened to stories with great interest. Between 1900 when Susan, the first Solley baby, was born, and 1935 when the last baby Edward was about ten years old, competition for natural self-entertainment was rare. They read for pleasure after they had studied their school work. They popped corn and parched peanuts.

It was pretty difficult for the girls to learn to sew and complete their articles as well and as fast as Sarah could, because since Sarah was an only child she had started learning all of this earlier in life, and she had spent less years in school than her girls. Therefore, she had had more time for this kind of thing. The regularity of Sarah's sewing had helped.

Aunt Pearl's Visit and Voting Rights for Colored People

When Sarah's half-sister Pearl came to visit them, the children always tried to be on their best behavior. The one thing which was not good, the children felt, and it was that Aunt Pearl never stayed long enough. They didn't have company often.

Always when Aunt Pearl came, the children who were available wanted to make a day of going in the wagon to the train to meet her. The wagon ride, when no work was involved, was always a pleasure trip. Old quilts on the floor of the wagon behind the two wagon spring seats made a fun ride to the train station. It had never been necessary for Jason and Sarah to explain the circumstances of Aunt Pearl to any of their children, for Aunt Pearl was just Aunt Pearl, a small, friendly, lovable woman. She seemed, to the Solley children, to love them almost as much as she loved her own. She was ready to join in their activities. If they were doing school work, she offered to help. When it was time for washing the dishes or churning the milk, she insisted on taking turns. She was always willing to give Sarah a hand.

Aunt Pearl admired Jason and Sarah. She would sometimes look longingly when her sister and that husband of hers paid such loving, caring attention to each other. Married so many years, and still could not stay away from each other for long. What a God-blessed woman! What a God-blessed man! She liked to visit because they and the children made the time so wonderful. The children did not seem to mind "sleeping together" so that Aunt Pearl could have the "company bed." That bed was not all that its name implied because the children kept coming and coming, and then that bed had long stopped being the "company bed."

When Aunt Pearl sometimes brought everybody something that she had made, it was a good time (maybe an apron, a pair of socks and on and on). She must have started working on these things as soon as she got back to her home after the last visit. She never was short of gifts. It must have taken lots of time to fix them.

One time Jason thought that Susan had let her Aunt Pearl take on too much of the dishwashing, so he called her and asked her to come with him to the smokehouse. She knew that something she had done did not please her pa. She could hardly wait. He chose the smokehouse because it was much closer to the main house than the barn. Jason explained very carefully why it was not good manners or good ethics (he had read enough to understand that word) to do it this way. He made her promise to go into the house and say, "I'm sorry, Aunt Pearl." He told her that she must never take unfair advantage of company or anyone else. It took away from her good side. His young gal was marched back into the main house to make everything right. That was the way of Jason. He was as serious and quiet in his way as Sarah was more outspoken in her way. They were raising good children though. They didn't go to church for nothing. They meant it for good, and they felt it showed in their children.

Jason was a praying man, and he always told his family, or anyone else for that matter, that he didn't believe in playing with God. Those were great big words and strong sincere words coming from Jason Solley's mouth. Everybody, his kinfolks, his friends, and his acquaintances who lived in the Plum Creek Valley area of the deep South and had any dealings with him, knew this. All that those words had really meant for Jason was that he was sincere. While he was quick to point out that he made many mistakes, he always added that they were what he called "honest mistakes." He was quick to make an apology.

When Jason had chastised his oldest gal about her treatment of Aunt Pearl, everything seemed brighter around their house. Aunt Pearl continued to enjoy herself. She especially enjoyed Joe Baker, the young boy that her sister Sarah had been reaching out to help. He had been changing and changing and all for good. The Solley household started to really like Joe because he was getting better all the time. The older colored people around that part of Plum Creek Valley began to say, "Good chillun like the Solleys sho' 'nuf can rub off on some other chilluns 'cause they be good influence on 'em." Of course, all the mamas and papas didn't want to hear remarks like that. Naturally, some were known to say things like, "The Solley chilluns got de big head 'cause da ma had all dem younguns and still can sew pretty clothes and look better than any ma has a right to look with that bigga bunch." Most of them, though, just wished they had Sarah's talent and her good heart. She sho' had a good heart.

Aunt Pearl's visit had been just a little longer than she stayed sometimes. She said she must get back home so she could vote. Yes, it was time to vote again. Colored folks were given a privilege with the 15th Amendment of the right to vote on February 3, 1870. Many of them had thought that the 14th Amendment would bring that privilege, but it was not clear enough on that point. The 15th, though, made it legally clear that Freedmen could now vote. Naturally, some people were not so happy about this, and thought because of so much illiteracy among colored people that they perhaps should not vote. Voting was such a great way to be able to have a say-so in the running of the things that affected freed people, as well as everybody else in the counties, states and the entire country. Freed people could exercise this right and begin to feel more like they counted for something in this country. They could feel a little more like their freedom spoke more than some words written on a piece of paper. The Solleys explained this to their children.

President McKinley's Assassination

Jason and Sarah would always try hard to take their many children into a learning situation. They would call them together to sit down to a family session. They figured if they picked cotton together, cut sugar cane together, and shelled corn off cobs together, they should be able to listen to their pa's family speeches together. They were encouraged by their ma to really listen good and take it all to heart, because no other colored man in Plum Creek Valley did more reading about what was going on than their own pa. Their own pa didn't get to go to Howard University in Washington, D.C. the way he wanted to, but he knew almost as much as some of those who did, she reckoned. When Sarah made her "Listen up, children" speech, everybody had to listen real good. They all did, too.

One night Jason told them about President William H. McKinley's assassination in 1901. He told them that he and their ma Sarah did not have to just read it in the history books to know it, because it had happened after they had been married almost three years. They had married in 1898. The children were just fascinated to hear that their parents had really been living way back then. Jason told them that he and their ma had heard that awful day called "Black Friday." Then Mindy, one of the younger girls had wanted to know why

Black Friday, and did it get its name after colored people? Couldn't it have been named colored Friday? Jason and Sarah smiled at each other first. Then Jason explained that the Black Friday did not have anything to do with people at all. It had to do with a horrible, terrible, awful and ugly day because the number one leader of the United States of America had been gunned down just like he was a mad-dog. He explained that it was done by someone who hated the President, or someone who didn't like the way the President led the country, or someone who was just plain crazy, or someone who accepted pay to do this because somebody else did not like the way the President was doing his job of presidenting. Jason had to admit to himself that the question of this young child meant that this child who had been born to him and his Sarah, could think. He wanted all of the children in this house to really think about things. Go all the way with their thinking is what Jason and Sarah were trying to teach.

Jason thought of one more thing for this part of their session. He asked the question, "Can either one of you tell us what number President McKinley was? No, better still, don't tell us if you do know, not now. Look it up in the library, and then write the answer down without telling anyone else. Then give your answer to your ma tomorrow night just before supper. Remember, if you already know the answer, you don't have to look. Just go write it down and hand it to her." Jason always enjoyed putting a little "thought-catching" into his sessions. He thought his Sarah was so good at making the children want to learn. He liked the way she made it all come alive. His Sarah!

Jason had a small "library" in the corner of the big front room, the sitting-bedroom. This was the Ma and Pa room at bedtime. The "library" consisted of every book that the white folk had ever given him, and also of any book he had ever been able to buy, and all of the best newspaper articles that were saved and pasted on cut cardboard squares. It also consisted of Sarah's old school readings and recitations. It had all the debate materials he had ever done and all of the orations that he had done since the first one. Sarah and Jason had encouraged their children to save any and all of their good work for the library. The library consisted of a homemade cabinet with shelves. There was a key for Sarah and one for Jason. The children had been allowed to use this precious library. It was deemed a privilege as well as a learning pleasure. None of the Solley bunch could use this reading material without "spic and span" clean hands or without a real show of interest and commitment. Everything in this library might not have been arranged by the Dewey Decimal System, but it was in order (order in that everything could be found easily and quickly). Neither Jason or Sarah would have allowed things in that little family library to be so "stirred up" that the next user could not find everything quickly.

Third Generation of Slave-Born Children: Work, Church, School, and the Meaning of Freedom

The Solleys were very intense about their children being able to acquire an ownership of dignity that had been denied them because of their closeness to the evils that slavery had bestowed upon them (their race, their lack of proper education, and their inability to earn enough money to live in better neighborhoods and have access to better schools). The official end of slavery did not allow many colored people to feel really free (free of the elements that held many of them fast). Jason and Sarah wanted their children to understand that they were living in the third generation of the 1858 and 1860 grandparents on Sarah's side of the family, the same generation of Jason's 1855 and 1857 grandparents. The Solleys meant to support and encourage their bunch with every bit of their being. Even though they all worked very hard in their own fields, woods, and pastures, it did not end there. They sometimes got into work trucks at 4:30 and 5 o'clock in the morning to go work in white well-to-do, and maybe not so well-to-do fields, hoeing and picking cotton, strawberries, and anything else growing. This, of course, was to supplement their meager farm earnings and help them to fulfill their dreams of a better life. None of them really intended to keep this kind of life for the rest of their life. They were encouraged to save every penny possible to help the family and themselves. This family held its head always high.

Work was not the only thing important going on. The Solleys were Sunday School and church goers. Since it would have been extremely difficult for this family to take full-body washtub baths each day, Sarah made sure that she gave all of the little ones their full baths on Saturday at bedtime. They all had to be clean, fresh and sweet for church. When she had finished with the hot water for them, more water had been drawn up from the well, and the big black wash pot in the yard and the small pot and kettle on the stoves had been filled and kept piping hot for the other family members. No body in Sarah's house escaped the Saturday night bath. Jason and the big boys took a washtub to an almost empty crib in the barn, and that's where their bathing was done in their very own private "bathroom." This worked just fine until the weather got cold. Then they used a small coal oil heater to keep warm while and after bathing.

Jason called his big boys together and did a "bath-taking conference." He asked a question, "What do we all need to know when washing ourselves in the barn?" Jim said, "We need to know that the cows and mules can look through these big cracks and see our nakedness. Then we may need to cover up our naked selves." With that, he laughed a big son-papa laugh. Everybody else caught his joke and laughed, too. However, Jason was ready to move on with the real answer, in his opinion, to a very serious question.

Ray said, "Pa, we know to be very, very careful and don't *ever* knock over our little space heater. Since it is so small and very light weight, this could happen. Then we could have a big coal oil fire from the little coal oil heater. Then we could burn the bar down; and there would go our corn for bread and feeding, then our peanuts for just parching and eating (maybe selling), and our hay and corn fodder to feed our livestock. It is important that we keep the heater far enough to the side that we cannot bump into it."

Everybody had been listening to Ray, the second oldest boy. Jason felt quite satisfied with that rational and sensible explanation. His method of questions and answers are sometimes just what they need to help them think. Yes, all of the Solley children should be thinkers. Jason knew this was the only way out (right thinking is the way to go up).

After Sarah had seen to it that everybody was washed satisfactorily, she took her own full-body bath that was so much better than her daily wash-ups. She felt so good to sit down in the big washtub and put her feet down to the wooden floor on a little hand-braided rug. This was surely the best time of Saturday. The children were all asleep, and she and her Jason had settled down in their own double bed. He still knew just how to reach out to pull her into his well-worked but strong tender arms. She felt that she was real blessed to love him this deeply after so much self giving to the children. Jason looked forward to this really special time, too. This would be a good night; Sarah still knew exactly how to make him feel proud to be a man.

The next day, Sunday, was a day to start in time to make Sunday School. Church service was held every other Sunday when their shared-time preacher would be there. In winter the stove had to be warmed up. When the church members and their babies and children came, the church was ready. Since they had no paid janitor, the men took turns sweeping the floor, dusting the seats, and just making everything ready before the crowd showed up. Since Jason was the Sunday School superintendent, he was careful to do exactly what he thought his job required. At 10 o'clock sharp he tapped the little bell on his table. This was to bring things to order. Things meaning everybody young and old got quiet, and hastened to their seats for the grand opening. Then after singing songs like *Come to Jesus, Come to Jesus* and *I Come to the Garden,* there would be prayer with everyone kneeling and closed eyes. They believed that this was the way it should be done (nobody standing or looking around the little country church in Plum Creek Valley). Everybody should be preparing to worship.

Sunday School lasted for about one hour. The teachers had almost always prepared their lessons well. The superintendent usually did not teach unless a teacher was very suddenly taken sick. Jason had always studied the general lesson, and he was also a Bible scholar. Therefore, he was never in a bind for something to bring to any class. The children really did enjoy having "Uncle" Jason, "Cuttin" Jason or "Mr." Jason come to help out if their teacher was not there or if the teacher happened to be late for a special reason. It had to be a special reason. It had to be a special reason because a small church in Plum Creek Valley was just as loved by God as any church in Chicago, St. Louis or Nashville, Tennessee, everyone knew.

When the bell was tapped once, the classes began to finish their last sentences, and when it was tapped twice, they prepared to put their collection envelopes in the big plate. Someone from a class did a short review of the lesson. The classes all listened to this review. The superintendent closed Sunday School. There was 15 minutes before the church service started. All the children were warned to run across the yard to the outdoor toilet to do their proper eliminations because there would be no running out to pee while the church was going (not unless somebody got really sick, really sick!).

When the preacher stood up to lead a song, it was time

for everybody to stand and sing. There was no choir. The whole church was the choir. Everybody knew or soon knew the songs that were sung at this church. When the preacher finished, there would be a collection taken. Before this started, the preacher explained for the 100th time or more that this giving should not be considered giving dues to the church or giving because God so needed it. He said that the giving was because the money really did belong to God. They were just putting in what was not their part anyway. Well, some people seemed to understand it at last. Others never seemed to understand it at all. They gave what they wanted.

When church was over and the hand-shaking was all done, some people loaded their children into their wagons and drove home. Other people walked home. Sometimes the preacher and his family got invited home for dinner with some of the members, but sometimes the preacher's wife was left to cook their own dinner. If they got invited to the Solley house, they knew before church that they were going. There were so many Solleys that Sarah had to plan to put an extra hen in the pot to make a whole lot more dumplings or cornbread dressing and make a bigger pot of mustard greens. Also, Sarah would use her real big cobbler pan to make a peach cobbler and use another one to make a plum cobbler. How in the world could she invite the preacher without these cobblers? The preachers were always glad to get invited to this house with all the children. They knew they would get these good things, but sometimes they forgot that some special effort on Sarah's and Jason's part and sacrifice on the children's part went into this wonderful, bountiful Sunday meal. Sarah always knew that except for the sugar, flour, vanilla flavor and other spices, just about all could be grown on their farm. She was so much like her ma, Mattie, in this way. Mattie believed a good piece of chicken and a good plum pudding or cobbler could go a long, long way in making somebody feel welcome in her house. Sarah had her ma's good heart, for sure. Mattie never did get tired of trying to lift somebody.

When the Solleys were going to have the preacher for dinner, Sarah would be the one to think first to ask Joe Baker's ma if he could come and eat with them. His ma and pa always seemed happy for this. Joe would exclaim, "Oh, thank you, ma'am, Miss Sarah. You sho' does cook good. I sho' does like to be 'vited to yo' house. I likes you an' Mr. Jason an' I sho' likes all yo' chillun. Dey sho' nuf is good chillun. I really try to be likes yo' chilluns. I'm gonna be like 'em!"

"You are so very welcome, Joe. We do like for you to come. We enjoy having you eat with us. Maybe sometime you can go fishing with us, too," Sarah said.

Joe exclaimed, "Could I? Could I go? I sho' do wants to go, Miss Sarah!"

"Sometime we'll see just how we can do this."

"Yes, ma'am! Yes, ma'am! I sho' does loves you, Miss Sarah!"

"I love you, too, Joe, and you getting to be such a good boy!"

Sarah knew that all of her family, from her and Jason all the way down, had a lot to learn 'bout knowing how to talk better. As she would listen to their young friend, Joe, she worried 'bout what to do to get this started. All the books that white people gave Jason, and all the newspapers and Rexall magazines that they got hold of had good-sounding writing. The writing looked different from the way a whole lot of colored folk still talked. She wanted to see what Jason could add to her idea. Now, she could hardly wait for supper to be over so they could talk about this. She thought fast. Sarah started right out, "Joe being around us so much makes me wonder 'cause his talking is really sweet now, but it is just so bad-bad English, I mean. He talks wusser than lots of us whose ma and pa and grandma and grandpa was born slaves. You got any ideas, Jason? What in the world can we do? Jason put his chin in his hand with his elbow on his chair arm. He thought and thought. Then he said, "Maybe we can start by saying right out to Joe and our children that we *have* to talk better if we want to be counted along with the people who never had the stains of slavery to deal with. We have to talk more like they do."

"That's a good idea, but where do we start?" Sarah said. She saw that this was not as easy as it looked.

"Well, since we know we want to talk and think so much better, we can read more. Our reading is in good English. We have to pay more attention to that. We need to help correct one another all the time," Jason said.

Now, that did sound pretty good, Sarah thought. "Since Joe is doing so much better, we should include him. He wants a whole lot to be more like us. He don't get much help at his house. Also, I hear that his ma and pa fuss and fight. I sho' do hope they don't do that, though," Sarah continued seriously. "We'll have our Solley family session and tell all of our children to start by correcting each other whenever they hear bad-sounding grammar. Joe is like one of our boys now. So he will get included when he is with us," Jason said.

This new idea to improve good sound thinking, and a better way of talking was accepted by all of the Solley group, and Joe was told about the plan. He was so glad that he had a part in all this. He kept improving in his school books, too. Jason became really interested in him because he saw talent in this boy. The more he was around Joe, he would be reminded of his brother Gilbert, who was a school teacher many miles away from Plum Creek Valley. They said he was a good teacher who taught the school children lots of arithmetic, grammar and history. Maybe Joe would one day be a teacher. Two of the Solley children wanted to be school teachers, they were saying. Jason and Sarah tried always to encourage all of their children. They knew their chances in this country to be full-time citizens were much better than ever before.

One day after supper the Solleys got a surprise. A wagon was coming up the road and pulled up under the big oak tree outside the yard. It was Joe Baker's ma and pa. They had never come a-calling before. Not ever in these years. They tied up the mules and got out of the wagon. Joe's pa got out first, and quickly went to the other side of the spring seat to help Joe's ma out. Now, that was sho' 'nuf a good sign of manners. All of the Freedmen did not yet learn to do this for their women riders. Sarah hurried to the end of the porch and met them right at the steps smiling.

"Come right in. Come right in!" she said. "We hopes we not in a bad time for y'all. We hopes you et yo' supper. We done et our supper. Then we just wanted to pay a little visit 'cause we preshate y'all treatin' Joe so good. We gotta say that Joe been so much mo' ready to go to all the things he 'spose to go to since he been with y'all's chillun. We thought it be right to come say it to yo' faces. Y'all's mighty fine peoples," Mrs. Baker said. She was a woman of bigness (big face, big body, and a big toothie smile). It was not at all unpleasant to meet her in the home. Sarah had never been quite this close to her before. She was a kind-speaking woman.

Mr. Baker shook Jason's hand and said quickly, "We glad we came to yo' house. We thought after supper might be a best time. We do thank y'all and all y'all's chilluns for being

Joe's acquaintance. You have helped him be a gooder boy. Oh yea, he sho' 'nuf a much gooder boy. He wants to go "off to school" and study to be a school teacher. We goin' try to encourage him much as we can. He got a good head on him. He jus need to put it to mo' good use. Mr. Jason, next time you do some oratin' round these parts, we sho' wants to know exactly what day or night and exactly what time. We keeps hearing that you read a whole lotsa white folks books. We heard that you keep yo' own "liberry." White folks 'round here don' have no "liberry" for slaves' chilluns and their chilluns, not yet. But maybes one day fo' the Good Lawd calls for me, I gits to see a colored "liberry" right here in ol' Plum Creek Valley, 'cause I ain't aiming to go nowhere to the Good Lawd anyways soon," he laughed.

Lawrence and Mattie did not invite their children to come in. The Bakers did not have Joe with them. This was all right because it was just the papas and the mamas this time. There would be other times for them all. This was a very good beginning. Lawrence answered Mr. Bakers request, saying, "When I speak again whether it's orating or debating on any subject, I will be sure to send you word by Joe or one of our boys."

Joe's pa said, "Well, I sho' does thank you so much. I'll be waiting with my wife."

In the meantime, Joe's ma had spied the very pretty quilt on the older Solleys' bed. She said to Sarah, "Do you do all that pretty quilt piecing and quilting yo'self?"

Sarah smiled and said quietly, I do all the quilt piecing, but I sometimes have "quilting bees" to help. Next time I have a quilting, would you like to come and eat some teacakes or gingerbread while quilting?"

Mrs. Baker's face lighted up as she answered quickly and

brightly, "Oh, I loves it that you asked me, and I sho' do aim to come when you lets me know."

"I will let you know. It may be a good while, but I won't forget. I look forward to the next quilting time," Sarah said brightly also.

After the Solleys had thanked the Bakers for coming and had seen the wagon go off into the early evening, they knew that this was the beginning of a new relationship and of a good one. Neither could imagine any truth in the gossip that the Bakers might fight. Mr. Baker, a rather small stature man, and Mrs. Baker, just the opposite, just didn't seem like fighting people. Both seemed rather eager, in a quiet way, to be in a new relationship with this couple that had so long been friends to their Joe. Jason said, "I sensed a kind of loneliness tonight in our 'company' that we enjoyed so much. I wonder why."

Sarah thought for a moment. Then she said, "They moved to Plum Creek Valley from another part of the deep South. If you notice, their dialect is harshly different from ours. Some people say that they talk "wusser" than most of us who grew up in these parts. Could that be the reason some colored folk here seem to think that the Bakers are below them? Could that be a reason why Joe would not act just right 'cause he felt sort of left out? Could that be a reason for some mean people to make up stories about them fighting each other? You know, some people can be so mean-hearted."

Jason answered, "You know, my Sarah, my sweet, smart, pretty girl, the girl who keeps helping me to know that she is the only woman I have ever loved; you have just the answer to my question. There is not a better answer that I could believe, than the one you just explained so well. Thank you, my dear, sweet Sarah." After that they met in the middle of the room and really hugged and hugged each other. They went to be among the children.

The children had done their own things. They were all glad that Ma and Pa had enjoyed their company, for they had learned to like Joe Baker a whole lot. He was such a likeable young fella. They hoped to have that company again. Joe was smart, too. Nona spoke and said, "Yes, Joe is so much smarter than lots of other boys I know. He has just got looked over a lot because of his speaking. He does not speak as good as some of the colored people who have lived in Plum Creek Valley all their lives. He spoke the colored folk way where he came from, but his grandparents and great-grandparents were born slaves, too. Folk need to remember things like that befo' they start to raise their noses up so high above the ground."

"Amen, amen," Charley chimed in.

Ray said, "Yeah, one of the big troubles with some of us, we think we are too big for our britches since we not slaves no mo', but if you ask me, we still got a long, long way to go. I want to be an automobile maker so that many folk can ride to places faster instead of having to go in the wagon, the hack or the buggy. They'll git you there, but the car is faster. Trouble is right now that they cost a lot of money, and most colored people don't make enough money to buy one. But just wait. Keep on picking extra cotton, cutting extra firewood and saving all of the money you can (not to buy the car yet, but to go to school some more). Get some more learning in yo' heads. Then some better jobs will be offered to ya'. That's how it gonna havta be done. I'm also trying to speak better grammar. Them white people with the good jobs don't talk the way so many of us still talking. We gots to hurry and get to learning everything faster and faster." Ray said all this as if he was orating like pa Jason.

After Sarah and Jason had listened patiently and with a whole lot of admiration, they looked at teach other in total agreement, and without saying one word to each other raised their four hands in applause. They clapped and they clapped for the three Solley children who had just shown their ma, pa and everybody in the house that they were learning to think straight and speak straight. Oh, yeah, there was plenty room left for improvement in all of it, but the start was looking so good. Applause from these two meant everything.

The Solleys started to get ready to go to bed. Jason said to them. "Listen here and give me an answer, just anybody. We had some unexpected company tonight! While it was real pleasant and we didn't happen to mind, what invention could now keep surprise visits from being a surprise?"

The children quickly chimed in a chorus, "Alexander Graham Bell's telephone!"

"That is just right!", said Pa Jason.

"But we'd have to have a telephone, and the *Bakers* would have to have a telephone, too," Louise yelled out loud.

Sarah said, "That is sho' right, too!"

The Solley children were working, going to their one-room school, and learning. They were having ups and they were having downs, but they were remembering that one day they would arrive at the place which they were traveling to. Ma Sarah and Pa Jason never let their children forget. "Know where you come from, know where you on your way to and you'll know when you get there." Jason and Sarah said this. They prayed to God at each meal, all through the day, and bedtime.

One-Room School and a Good Teacher, Miss Blakeman

Attending their one-room school meant that the Solley children had access to the school "library." They were able to become friends with their teacher (one teacher per school term per year). Their really good teachers were like second parents. They shared the things with the children that they didn't have, but wanted to help the children know the kinds of things they'd learn in a big city school. They wanted them to leave here ready for high school.

Solley children enjoyed their school because they could listen to their own class discussions, and they could listen to other classes even higher than they. They really could learn more that way. They all listened because anyone of them might be called upon by Ma Solley or Pa Solley to tell something very specific about what he or she had learned that day at school. The children never did know what would be asked or who would be asked. This really kept them on their toes.

"Tell me why you like or don't like the Grimm Brothers," or to some of the older children it might be. "What did the 15th Amendment do for colored people?" Pa Solley could and did ask questions just like a teacher. He had made very sure that he knew that these questions had been discussed in class before he asked. Ma Solley remembered her recitations and her reviewings of Nathaniel Hawthone's works before she was finished with her fifth grade education. She wanted to be sure that her children knew as much finishing the sixth or seventh grade as she had known finishing fifth grade.

Ma would ask, "Can you spell extraordinary?" She would be speaking to seventh grade Ray or to sixth grade Gerald. She waited patiently for the correct answer.

Gerald answered, "Oh, Ma, I could spell that two or three years ago."

Sarah would say, "Well, just spell it right now and I'll be happy."

Gerald said, "Oh, aw right, Ma. I'll spell it!" Then he would spell it incorrectly.

Miss Jerry Blakeman was one of the best one-room teachers in Plum Creek Valley country. She taught the children so many things other than what was exactly in their school books. She would say to the whole school of first to eighth graders. "Now, everybody here is in a Negro school. Everybody here must know about other Negroes who made contributions to help us be more like we're striving to be. Is that right, school?"

"Yes, Miss Blakeman, that sho' 'nuf is right!" one of the students called out, real loud.

Miss Blakeman would say, "Is that the correct answer, school?"

They would answer in a chorus, "Yes, Miss Blakeman!"

She would continue, "No, that answer was incorrect! Does anybody know why I said that the answer given was incorrect?" Miss Blakeman asked the school again. Nobody could give the answer that Miss Blakeman was still seeking. Miss Blakeman continued, "Would you stand, please, the student who gave the answer." Nobody did what was asked! Nobody stood! Miss Blakeman looked all around, up and down the rows of desks, but nobody was standing (nobody at all!). Miss

Blakeman said, "Well, somebody answered that questions, but when I said it was incorrect before the whole school, that person has decided to be a coward. We all know what a coward says about a person. That one word coward identifies that person as being scared, as being really little in spirit, as being ashamed, and as being worst of all, what he or she would not want their mother or their father to know about because they would also be ashamed. They had tried so hard to teach the right way from the wrong way. So let's start again, and we can do it right this time. Then nobody will have to go home ashamed after school or ashamed before school is out. So, we fix it by asking the student who gave that first answer to come forward."

Charley Solley got up and went up to the teacher. He said, "I thought I gave the correct answer."

Miss Blakeman said, "You surely did!" *Everybody* then raised up in their seats. Nobody seemed to understand. Miss Blakeman said, "Charley, you are smart, but you revoked your correct answer when you added that last incorrect part. You added something we all learned two weeks ago was incorrect for anybody and everybody. You said, 'Sho' 'nuf is right.' Now, that is what made your correct answer an incorrect answer. Understand, everybody?"

They all answered, "Yes, Miss Blakeman, we understand."

She said, "Well, this might have seemed like a lot of time to learn one thing, but you will all see how important it is to speak correctly as you go along. Colored people can miss good jobs or other worthwhile things in this country because of poor grammar. Colored people need to learn this and really live by it because it is one way to move up to where you are trying to get to. After colored people became free colored people, we are learning to work harder. Maybe not the cotton field or the plum thickets or a white person's washtubs, but for ourselves. We must work to be all that we can be, and we cannot do this as young people, without a good home, and a good church, and a good school. It's going to take all three of these elements to help us be what we should be. We cannot afford to let this new freedom slip away from us because we are just not diligent enough!"

Miss Blakeman added, "Now, nobody here in our school today has anything to go home ashamed of."

When Miss Blakeman had finished her speech, one student raised her hand. It was a student who was, as a rule, pretty quiet. She was a daughter of one of Jason Solley's friends. Her name was Sylvia Compton.

Miss Blakeman recognized her high-held hand and said, "What do you want to say, Sylvia?"

Sylvia said, "I want to add one more thing to the three things you just told us we must have as colored young people to be all that we should be. Besides good home, good church and good school, I think we should add good teacher because our teacher, Miss Blakeman, carries us far, far beyond some of the things we study in our school books. Therefore, let the whole school just add our good teacher to that list." With those words the whole school stood up and clapped their hands so happily. Sylvia was quiet, and Sylvia was deep. Sylvia was right.

"Thank you, Sylvia, and the whole school," Miss Blakeman said.

After this the one-room school was dismissed. Miss Blakeman walked slowly to her rented room. She enjoyed teaching these children who needed so much to learn. She looked up at the trees and the birds flying over. She smelled the variety of flowers with the beautiful array of colors. She felt the warm sun on her back, and she was happy. She found herself saying a silent prayer as she often did for her school students. They had a long road ahead of them. She just wanted to be re-assigned to Pine Hill Grade School. When these students finished the eighth grade, she wanted them to be ready for high school. She prayed aloud. "Lord, please help me be a good teacher."

Cotton Picking and Home-Schooling

When most of the Plum Creek Valley colored children got a chance to go to their one-room school it was after cotton-picking time was over in the fall and after cotton-hoeing time was completed in the spring. That was one reason why their school terms, even though very short, were sometimes split into two parts. Cotton was considered to be "King Cotton." Colored children, as well as older people, worked hard to produce cotton. Not only did U.S.A. use a lot of cotton, England was the single largest user of the South's production of the "King." Colored folks were the biggest pickers.

September sun can be awfully hot in the deep South, but colored school children could not afford to do too much concentration on it. They had to pick that cotton. Most of them would have had questions (questions that did not get them out of the cotton field, though). Some of them would ask questions out loud just like Edward Solley, who said, "Why we out here in this ole hot, hot sun picking this ole cotton when the white children are going getting up eating their breakfast and going to school? We need to be learning, too, so that we can get out of this cotton!"

His sister Mindy listened to her brother and agreed wholehearted by saying, "Yes, I hate to see those children out playing in the shade just looking so cool and pretty. They don't look all hot and sweaty and smelly like we are right now! What other kinds of jobs can we get to do if we can't learn nothing but cotton picking and such? I think we got to remember what Ma and Pa tell us all the time to study harder 'cause we go to school shorter. One day we go off to high school when we finish these eight grades just like Jim did and just like Susan did. After the four years of high school, then maybe we can get into a college. Pa always wanted to go to Howard University, but Grandpa died before he got a chance to go. His sister, the youngest one, went to college for a while. She's dead now though. Everybody said she was so proper, too. She was a nurse, and when she got sick, she couldn't help herself like she had helped other people, and she just died off."

Mindy had talked so long she had forgotten to keep picking cotton fast. She was getting farther and farther behind picking her row of cotton. Edward could not pick fast at all. Therefore, he was falling even farther behind. Somebody called out from way up in the front rows of cotton and hollered loud, "You slow-pokeys better stop all that cotton field day dreaming. You'll never be a doctor or a school teacher or anything else but a cotton picker if you don't stop talking and get to work!" Some of the others started hollering and snickering, "Cotton pickers, cotton pickers, all you 'cullard chillun' cotton pickers. Got to pick harder, and git blacker, you po' little cullard chillun' cotton pickers. In the sun longer, but yo' backs gittin stronger. You po' little 'cullard chillun' cotton pickers." As the little made-up tune came to a close, everybody knew it was a good cotton-picking laugh-up time. They all laughed. Though they laughed, they did not miss a word of the meaning. They laughed to lighten the work.

Some women over in some other fields had to bring their

babies to the cotton fields. They put big-billed bonnets on the babies to keep the hot sun off. Then they put the babies, securely fastened, on top of their long, long cotton sacks. Poor little babies! Poor women! When the children would go home and tell their ma Sarah about what they saw, Sarah would say, "Oh Lawd, have mercy! Lawd, have mercy! Where in the world are their husbands? Can't they do no better job than that taking care of their wives and little biddie babies?" Sarah had never gone into the field since she married her Jason. He promised that the garden vegetables, the peach orchard, the other fruit trees and the flower yard, plus all their babies would be more than enough to keep his Sarah more than busy. He never did forget his promise. If he came home for dinner time (noon time) and he didn't see her, he went or sent someone to the garden. She'd sometimes cook and then run back to the garden. Sometime she'd forget the exact time and would be on the back porch peeling peaches or stringing beans. She did a whole lot of canning and drying and preserving of fruits and vegetables. One of the boys had to build more shelves in the backroom for the Mason fruit jars. When the girls were away from the field, they helped Sarah with all of this. Sarah would say, "Come on and let's get these peaches on top of the barn to dry today. It's going to be real hot." The dried fruits were for those winter meals. They helped make breakfast, and they made dinners more filling. They filled the empty spaces in all the Solley stomachs that the fresh plums, peaches and pears were not there to fill. They were needed things. Sarah made sure they had them.

    The Solley children saw a lot of things that made them know exactly what their ma and pa were always trying to tell them. Being free does not mean being free of the responsibilities that will make life worth living. Jason talked a lot about this newly found freedom to the children. He often said things like, "I'm free now, but what does this really mean? I'm free to sit down under the oak tree in the corner of the yard all day long, and listen to the birds sing or watch the little busy ants storing up food for winter? If I use my freedom that way, am I really free?" When Pa asked a simple-sounding question, all the Solley children knew he was expecting an answer that was not so simple after all. They were supposed to think about the long-range implications of their answer. Sometimes two or three different answers would come. Jason waited to hear each answer. He was teaching.

Mindy said, "Pa, while you sitting there enjoying your freedom, the mules have not been fed, the corn has not been plowed, the dry corn did not get taken to the grist mill, and Ma is mad at you. Yes, she's real mad! What kind of freedom is that?"

Gerald said, "Pa, are you really enjoying being free when us boys are sawing the fire wood, cutting the cane and shoveling up the cow and mule manure in the barnyard? Would you rather we be free to leave it and step in it?"

Charley chimed in with, "Pa, are you feeling right just enjoying your freedom while Ma is busy making a dress for Sophie to wear to the Sunday School program and making some britches for Claude to wear? Those are enough for now."

Jason had smiled to himself as he listened. Then Jason made his answer to his children like this. Jason said slowly, "Everyone of you just showed me that you understand about the cost of freedom. Freedom, while feeling real good, comes with a cost, a price. It is not really freedom if we fail to use it, and just abuse it. There is a right time to sit under the oak tree, and there is a time not sit at all. We have to learn how to use our heads. We have to think and read (not just our school books either). What do I mean when I say the thing about not just our school books?"

Hazel spoke up fast, "Pa, don't you mean we have to read our Holy Bible, too, because Ma reads some of it every day before she cooks or go feed the chickens. She gets down her knees beside y'all's bed and say her daily prayers to the Good Lord. All of us know that we can't disturb her then. Ma calls this time of the day 'getting her strength' and being thankful. Pa, you do yours in the crib."

Jason was happy that Hazel, his fifth gal, had just given the right answer. He said to her and all who were there, "Hazel, you got that just right. I am proud of all of you. Keep up the good way of thinking about things. Freedom is not freedom without the good Lord's strength and power. He can help us make the right decisions."

Susan said, "Pa, everybody in this Solley house knows that you go to a corn crib in the barn every morning and give your thanks to God and also 'get your strength.' You pray before we all eat, too. I guess everybody knows that we can't do nothing much unless we give our thanks and 'get our strength.' "

Questions and Answers about Sharecropping

The Solley children, especially the younger ones, did not understand what "sharecropping" really meant. The older ones partially understood it. They understood that it didn't sound good at all. They wouldn't like it. Mark explained, "Some of the children in my grade at school live on sharecropping farms. My friend told me that his pa does not own the fields they plant in. He does not own the mules that plow the cotton, corn and peas. Even the cotton house where they store the cotton to take to the cotton gin does not belong to his pa."

"Why do they live on somebody else's farm, and whose house is it then, that they live in?" Edward wanted to know.

"It sho' don't sound like a good way to live." Edward looked up again from studying some spelling words to say. Then he added, "Why don't we ask Pa. He will be able to tell us. If Pa can't tell us, then maybe Ma will know. If Ma don't know, I'll ask Miss Blakeman when I go to school. She'll know. Our teacher knows everything (just everything, I believe). The children were now stirred up about this sharecropping stuff. They could hardly wait for Pa to come back from the grist mill. He went to take two bushels of dry shelled corn, so it could be ground into cornmeal to make those big pans of cornbread for dinner and supper. Pa would have some of the corn ground real course for the chickens, and especially the chickens that Ma kept in her chicken coops for cooking and eating right away. Now everybody would be waiting for Pa to get in from the mill. They wanted some answers and quick.

Mark said, "Well, look like I started something that I couldn't finish explaining, sharecropping. I am gonna look down the lane to see if Pa is coming. Since Pa wasn't coming yet, every body let this subject drop for now and went about the business of whatever he or she was doing.

When the wagon rolled up, Mark ran out to meet Pa. He couldn't wait any longer now. So he started right out, "Pa, we want to understand real, real good about sharecropping. Tell us why somebody would give away part of the stuff they had worked hard for? Give it away to some white man."

Jason said, "Just wait a minute. Wait a minute. Let me get our cornmeal and the chicken's corn feed out of the wagon." Once all that was done he came into the house.

"Where's Sarah?" Jason inquired.

"She went to take care of Miss Sadie and the new little baby 'cause they both kinda sick. She said she needed to go herself for this visit. That's the reason she didn't send one of us. She said to tell you she wouldn't be gone long though," Mark said.

After Jason had hung his jacket and hat on their nails, he sat down and said, "Now for the question of this sharecropping. Even though colored farmers are not slaves anymore, that doesn't mean that they all have the ownership of the houses they are living in, or the farmland they are working, or the mules they are using to pull the plows. Some people have to give half of whatever they're able to grow on the land they live on to the white owner of the land because the owner furnishes the little two-room shack house, the land, the mules to pull the plow, the garden to grow some vegetables, and all that. The colored farmer doesn't own anything. Therefore, the agreement to give half of whatever the crops yielded was the only way for some colored freedman to live until he could save or borrow enough to have his own farm. If these farmers had a really good year, they just might be able to save a little from their half, but most of the time they could just barely get by. This meant that they stayed 'in the hole,' so to speak, for a long, long time. The colored farmers who were able to somehow get a piece of land to call their own could get a little farther ahead faster. Some of the young men who get married real early and don't try to stay in school have no other way to go. So they end up with a young wife, three or four babies, and sharecropping. Then it's such a hard life because there seems to be no way out for them now. The young wives have to take the babies to the field with them sometimes. They may have a young sister to stay in the cotton house not far away with the baby. Sometimes the baby was left on a pallet under a big shade tree. Sometimes the young wives carried on her back her little baby in a swing-like canvass with a homemade makeshift cover protection from the sun. So, you see that sharecropping can be a really hard life. It's not the kind of living your ma and me want for you. You don't want that for your children," Jason ended.

Mindy had been really listening hard. She was thinking about the young wives who should have still been going to school having such a work-hard bad time. She was also wondering if the young husbands didn't wish that they had gone on to high school and maybe college before all this. She kept hearing that you could work your way through school after grade school. She expected those young mamas and papas wish they had tried that first. It sounds hard, but not hard for life. All of the children who were there listening had gotten some thought-provoking ears full.

One more question came to Pa about all of this. It was from Mindy who asked, "Pa, why don't we have to sharecrop? Is it because we have a very smart pa and ma or what?"

Jason thought for a long moment, and then he said, "I am the baby of the family. Your uncle Gilbert, my oldest brother, was a country school teacher. White people liked him because he knew how to act like they thought a colored man should act. He was what they called, very bright. They gave him every advantage they could. He did well by his family. I think I tried to be like him. My pa, your grandpa, died before I got all the schooling I wanted. I was needed at home, and I kept reading, studying, mathematics, history, etc. I started to be on the local colored people's debate team. I loved to stand up on stage and debate government issues, historical questions, etc. Then I saw a young girl at a special school program. She looked like a young African princess. She did her recitations so well. I wanted to make her acquaintance. I was not quite sure how to do it. So I went to her teacher, who said so many things about this young lady that truly did interest me. She encouraged me to seek her out and to get her parents' permission to see her. It all worked out so well and a few years later I married her."

"Oh, Pa, what a pretty story with such a nice ending," Louise yelled out.

Jason didn't let it end right there. So he said, "Listen up, you Solley younguns. Louise was right about almost half of what she said. Yes, I agree that it's a pretty story. I see that more and more each day, but the ending has not come yet. I have faith in God that it will be nice. There is so much more of this story to come."

Just then Sarah came dashing breathlessly through the back door. It was closer coming that way, and she was sure ready to be at home. Even though the trip didn't take that long and she liked taking Sadie and the baby hot chicken soup and a bowl of yellow plum cobbler, being back was so good. She went straight over to where Jason was sitting and kissed the very top of his head. Jason looked up and smiled while looking right into Sarah's eyes. It was so amazing the number of years and the number of children between them that they still displayed that special spark between them. They gave God credit.

World War I

World War I with Austria-Hungary against Russia broke out July 28, 1914, and started to involve the U.S.A.. Wars always are a great cause of apprehension and much concern no matter who is the cause factor. This war was no different. The U.S.A. did become involved. Many of our soldiers were killed or maimed. Some returned with no visible physical scars, but were suffering from the after-effects of being gassed. For some it was a periodic puffing/swelling of the abdomen. This could not be hidden very well. Some other things could and did remain unseen with the U.S.A. soldiers. World War I frightened the U.S.A. It left its black stain. Deaths, those stains could never be erased.

Jason had some friends who had to enlist and be called to active duty. He missed that. He was about 39 years old and was the father of eight children. He was not enlisted for that war. Sarah did not want to be guilty of not being patriotic, but she was so happy that Jason was not needed in this war. She needed him more to help her with their big family that the Good Lord had so graciously given them. Sarah and Jason spent much time on their knees praying for all the soldiers and their families which they'd left behind.

During the war, the Solley babies showed no desire to stop coming. Sarah was just as vigorous and busy as ever, and brought two more little Solleys into the world. She and Jason prayed harder for all the mamas and papas who had sons serving in the war. They tried to imagine what that must feel like for them and for the sons in the war way across the big ocean so far from home. Although they went to Sunday School and church with all the children each Sunday, they didn't forget to pray before every meal at home for the soldiers.

Jason would also remind the children of things to be thankful for and of things *not* to ask God for. One day Susan was praying to God to give her a new dress and new shoes to match for a special Sunday School program. Just a week before, she had balked at going to do some ironing and scrubbing for a white neighbor two miles up the road. She had made an excuse to not go. Jason said to her, "Susan, don't you feel guilty trying to use God's goodness for your laziness?"

Susan answered, "Pa, what you talking about?"

"Remember last week when you could have gone to Miss Simpson's house to iron and scrub? You made a poor, poor excuse not to go. You forgot that you were gonna need some money to buy yard goods for a dress and shoes. You hear us to talking about trusting God for things, don't you?"

"Yessuh, Pa, you and Ma always tell us to trust God for *everything!*"

"Trusting God does not mean for us to ask him to give us things that he clearly makes a way for us to get ourselves. When he makes a way and we are just too trifling to take him up on it, then it is our own fault. So now, you ought to be ashamed of yourself. Try to always remember this. I'm not going to give you the money I saved up for hard times. Your ma is not going to give you what she saved from selling eggs, green beans, etc. Therefore, you may not get another opportunity to have a new dress and shoes for the program."

Susan sat with her head down for a moment. Then she looked with great determination at her pa, and she said, "Thank you, Pa, for making my big mistake so plain for me to see. I wouldn't want to take Ma's savings or yours even if you offered it to me. I was wrong. Now, do you think I could tell God about this, and ask him for another chance to iron, scrub or something?"

Jason answered, "I'm glad you see my point. I am sure that God is even more pleased with you. He likes it when we see our wrong and try to correct it. Now, trust him to help you get a job real soon. If you don't get it, maybe you didn't have to have what you wanted. Let's see."

Just then Sarah came rushing in to say that she had just spotted a hummingbird fluttering its tiny wings over some of her yellow rosebuds in the front yard. She asked if the baby had been sleeping all the time she was working in the flowers. She looked at their sleeping baby and said, "The good Lord sho 'nuf is good. He lets us love, work and pray."

1918 Influenza Epidemic

Sarah and Jason, like thousands and thousands of Americans, were glad when World War I came to a close in 1918, but they didn't know the devastation that was heading their way. The influenza epidemic of 1918, which lasted about two years, came like a black storm. It made the people it attacked so very, very ill. Some families had been hit hard because of the evils of the war. Then right on the heels of that, this terrible illness struck some of the same families that were healing from the war. It was estimated that 28% of all Americans died from the fall of 1918 to 1920, bringing the total to approximately 175,000 persons. This was a huge devastation for the U.S. population at that time.

The Solley family could not escape this epidemic. Sarah and several of the children got sick. They had not had flu shots back then, and they depended on home remedies. No doctor came out those country roads of Plum Creek Valley to see the Solleys. They depended on medicines from the drugstore and home remedies. Jason made catnip tea, sage tea, horehound tea, and the most famous tea of all, cow-chip tea. Cow-chip tea would make people living in the twentieth century squirm just to envision it. It was made from sun-dried cow manure and boiling hot water. It was sweetened with molasses or honey. It was said by some that every time the patient became really thirsty, this tea was given. Sarah told people after she got well, "My children and me are living to talk about that terrible flu because we had cows. Our cows was what saved our lives. Thank God for our cows."

Jason made so much tea until he could only thank God for all of the teas and all of the chicken soup and anything else which helped to get the sick Solleys well. He said again and again, "If the cow-chip tea did the healing for my family, I don't mind thanking our cows for being our cows, but I sure do thank the Lord for what I *know* he did."

The Solleys lost relatives and friends (colored and white) to the influenza epidemic. They never forgot to thank God for saving them. Also, they remembered to ask God to comfort and strengthen all of the grieving people of America and help them to start again. Yes, start again, because World War I and that terrible influenza really took their toll.

Solley Children

The work around the Solley house and field was carefully divided and re-divided. Some of the older boys had learned to help Jason plow, cut wood, saw wood and harvest corn. They got so they could do it just as well as he could. When one of the older boys went off to school and another one went off to the big city, Jason trained the next oldest ones to do the same type things. Sarah had taught the oldest girls to cook, wash and clean the floors. Washing the clothes meant drawing up water from the well to fill the pots and tubs. Then the clothes were rubbed on a rub-board, boiled, rinsed and hung out on lines to dry just as in their grandparents' time.

Susan complained one day real loud, "Ma, Nona is slowing around when she should be hanging the clothes on the line. I have a lot of them ready for her to hang. Tell her to stop fooling around. I want to get through and sew on my new skirt!"

Nona called out, "Ma, I'm not slowing around; it is my day to wash breakfast dishes and I had to finish up. Then I scoured the kitchen floor. Tell Susan to stop pestering me. I'm hurrying all I can. Susan is a big pest! A pest!!"

Sarah came to the wash place in the back yard. She stood very still. For a moment she did not say one word. She looked from one of her big girls to the other. Then she quietly spoke,

"You two girls need to learn to work together without squabbling. This job has to be done, and right now the two of you are the ones to do it. So, make it easy on yourselves and do the right thing. One day each one of you will have your own house, your own husband, your own children, and your own washing to do. It is good that you are getting some real practice while you are with your ma and pa. Let me tell you that I learned everything that I knew about housekeeping with your Grandma Mattie, and I did not grow up with sisters and brothers like you. Since you have to learn together, just make it sweet and easy. Be thankful that you have each other to share with. This is not the first time I have had to give you a talk about this kind of thing. Am I right, girls? It's time to start really listening."

Susan answered very meekly, "Yes, Ma, you do always tell us right. We both just need to listen harder, I say."

Nona made an ugly face at Susan. She said, "Susan, you speak for yourself about both of us needing to listen. I *do* listen! You just want to boss me around like you my ma cause you the oldest. Yes, Ma, you do always tell us right."

As the Solley children got older and left home for higher education or city jobs or getting married, the younger ones became bolder in their quest for understanding their way of life, as opposed to the way of life they saw with their white friends and neighbors, and the ones they saw when they went to town. The younger children were more verbal and inquisitive as their parents got older.

Hazel had noticed that Pa called the white men Mr. Smith or Mr. Johnson, while they and all of their friends called her pa just plain Jason. She needed to know the answer. One day she decided to stop wondering about this and just come straight out and ask Pa. She said, "Pa, can you please tell me why you are so polite-like to Mr. Smith and Mr. Johnson. You don't call them by their first names like they do you. Why is that, Pa?"

Jason wanted to answer this question with as much clarity as he could. This made him think as he had to do when he was working with his debate team. So Jason walked up to Hazel and put his hand on her head. He prayed a silent prayer to give his answer just right. He wanted her to really understand that there was no animosity between them that caused this difference in addressing one another. He wanted to help her understand. He took his hand off her head and he said, "Hazel, let's sit down. Let me see if I can help you understand that this way we address each other has absolutely nothing to do with how we feel about each other. I guess you are seeing this as a fact: They are not respecting my pa like he is respecting them. But no, this is not what is going on here. This way of talking to each other started a long, long time ago when colored people were slaves of white people. Remember, all white people did not own slaves. Some were not wealthy enough to buy slaves. The ones who owned slaves could talk to them just like they were their servants, and therefore, not their equal. So as the masters spoke to the slaves like the servants that they were, they made sure that they spoke to the slaves in such a way that the slave could never ever forget his place with his master. The slave could never forget that his master was not nor ever would be his equal. Now, that brings us to today. It is hard to break old ways of life and old habits and old ways of seeing things that are so deeply imbedded in us. Sometimes we find it to our advantage to keep doing things the way we used to do them. The white men who were slave owners or descendants of slave-owners may be doing this kind of greeting out of age-old habits. Then it just might be easier to say things the old way because it may get what is wanted faster. The colored man might, without realizing it, still be feeling that he needs to continue in the old slave modes instead of holding for the change that might not get him nearly as much as he would get while trying to act like an equal. Yes, in the sight of God he is an equal. He was always an equal. Now, the colored man is trying to make a new place for himself. He is thinking about his family. He does want them to have a good place. All of this is saying that the colored man has more to lose if he is not careful. He can lose before he really gets if he is not careful. Even the white men who did not own slaves can speak to colored men the same way the others would, simply because they are white. Colored people don't go around asking any of them if their parents or grandparents owned slaves. So, as the old saying goes, they can ride in on the coattails of the advantages the real slave owners had."

Jason stopped there, and he looked at his daughter who was looking and listening as though she did not want to miss a single word. She had not thought of it this way. Then Hazel finally spoke, "Pa, it's a terrible shame that you have not written this down for not only all of the Solley children to read, but for a whole lot of colored people and white people to read. You could help a whole bunch of people to understand this thing. I'm sure so many colored and white people need to understand the real meaning of this great big thing that stands up so big and tall between them. Pa, even if you don't write this down, promise that you tell all of the Solleys. Then maybe you can find a real smart way to say it in one of your orations. I'm sure a lot of people could use this explanation, and maybe it will help coloreds and whites to live together better."

Jason was elated that Hazel had truly been listening. It did seem like she understood or thought she understood everything that he tried so hard to explain. He felt satisfied anyway. He turned his head up towards heaven and said out loud, "Thank you for this, dear God." He would take his daughter's advice and find a way to help some others with this same unasked question. There is nothing that he knew of which could take the place of better understanding in all things. Yes, better understanding is important.

Ku Klux Klan

A post Civil War Society called the Ku Klux Klan which advocated white supremacy had made itself known, and it was feared by colored people especially in the deep South. Sarah and Jason sat in the springseat of their wagon as they rode to town, and they talked seriously to each other about this. Ordinarily, this should have been a carefree pleasure trip for just the two of them as they left the children at home. However, they were now feeling stirred up and fearful. They had read some bad news in the newspaper about the Ku Klux Klan's activities against colored people. Also, some people had reported that they had actually been close enough to see a cross burning in somebody's yard. They reported that when they saw this in their wagon they were so scared that they turned their wagon right around to run quickly away. They had actually been so scared that they beat the mules unmercifully to make them hurry, hurry as fast as possible away from the scene. All they could think of was to not be spotted by these people. They did not want to come anywhere close to this group of people. They did not want to do anything that would make these people mad. Some people just tried to stay off any lonely road or trail. They had heard so many different kinds of stories about the Ku Klux Klan until they just didn't know how to think with any reason about them. People were saying all kinds of things. Some believed one could be caught and beaten or hung up on a tree limb for no other reason than that you were colored. Because you were colored, you must be taught some lessons about not thinking you were as good as white people. This was really getting the Plum Creek Valley colored folk unhappy. They were frightened almost beyond reason.

As the wagon wheels rolled over the rocks and dry dirt, the Solleys should have been happy for their day out to town. This should be a free day because the children who were still at home had been given their directives. They knew to stay in the yard and to venture no farther away than the barnyard until their parents returned home. Yet the Solleys felt not as carefree and happy as they should have been feeling.

Jason reached over and, without saying a single word to Sarah, patted her on her lap. She looked at him and smiled. Then she said, "If you could wash all of this Klan dirt away from all of this Valley and all of this post-war country, I know that you would have already done it, Jason. So, let's do what we always know we have to do, but instead of waiting for family gathering tonight, let's you and me pray right now.

Jason pulled on the mules' reins and steered them to the side of the road. He looked at Sarah. Sarah looked at him. They bowed their heads. For a moment all was quiet. Then almost at the same instance, they looked at each other and smiled. This time she reached over and touched his hand. He made a slight mule reins jerk to start and said, "Giddya yup." The mules stepped back onto the graveled road and went toward town. After watching the birds flying from tree to tree, the rabbits hopping through the bushes, the wild flowers' pretty colors, and even a buzzard circling and circling over some vulture on the ground not far away, the Solleys rode with a renewed spirit.

As the town of Fall Point came into view, the Solleys' spirits brightened more. They would enjoy this little town trip outing. Jason's special treat was bologna, loose crackers, strawberry soda water, cheese and crackers and peppermint stick candy. They found their favorite bench, sat down, opened their little brown paper sacks, said the blessings and ate with relish. This time was their rare special time out. They always enjoyed it. It was a time of renewal.

The Solley children at home thought of the welcome they would give Ma and Pa when they returned from town. They could look forward to getting some small treat like rock candy. Everybody would get a few balls of rock candy, since candy did not find its way into the Solley house often.

A Well-Respected Colored Man

Even though Sarah and Jason had allowed themselves the luxury of letting go of their concern about the Ku Klux Klan for a time, there was still new news from time to time which made them know it was a very real issue. It seemed that some of the concerns that the white supremacy group had been having was Black Insurrection and of Black Power at the polls. Those things at one time were not a worry for whites. The KKK wanted to control politics and not let the Freedmen in on this. They wanted to scare colored folk away by any means that they felt they could try and get away with. Around 1915 the second KKK was formed. They tried to make very sure that what had been started was reinforced, so to speak, especially politics.

Jason and Sarah wanted to be safe, and yet they wanted to be good citizens. So they made sure they accepted every opportunity to vote. Jason felt that they had to stand tall. Jason said to Sarah, "We have to keep asking God to protect us because we cannot let ourselves be frightened out of our rights and the rights of our children. Colored folk have been trampled down too long. It's time to take a stand."

Sarah answered him slowly. She said, "Jason, you are a well-respected colored man in Plum Creek Valley. You have always read so much and have been given so many good books by white men, you have orated a lot, and you have debated a whole lot. Now is your time to use some of that learning to encourage your colored people to stick close together and do what is the right thing to do. I believe these white men in and around Plum Creek Valley will be on your side all the way. Jason, we can't run too scared to try to get what is rightfully ours. We must not let the KKK scare us to death. I do mean death."

Jason answered with these words, "My Sarah, my Sarah, I have to agree with everything you have said. I don't want to do any less than what you and some others will expect of me. I must now stand up."

It was said that the KKK was formed in Tennessee. Plum Creek Valley was in KKK country. It extended far. When Jason talked to his family about the evils of the KKK, he tried to make sure that the children all understood what he was saying about fear and what fear can do to harm them in the long run. He tried to say that fear should not control them. He would say, "I don't want you to throw away your good sense that God gave you because you are scared when you ought to be standing up for something. Yet I don't want you to fail to use your good sense when you should back away from something. Sometimes, I admit, it's hard to know all by yourself which way to go. Remember that God can help you get your right directions. You have to lean on him when you can't figure it out. Right now we know that we colored folks' parents, grandparents and great-grandparents did not have certain rights. We must not be frightened out of ours because it was really God who delivered us from slavery. We must remember this."

Jason Solley was a dynamic leader in the colored community throughout the Pine Hill Grade School community. He was an eminent community personality. He was the school board president, Sunday School superintendent, a Masonic Lodge continual leader. He was a man of great integrity who did not reach his full potential because more formal education was denied him through no fault of his own. However, this man was undaunted. He continued to struggle against great odds to help his creative, talented wife Sarah raise 14 children in a respectable manner. There were ten young Solleys by the end of World War I. Four more were welcomed between 1918, when the war ended, and 1925, when the last Solley baby boy came to join this family. By now Sarah was a 46-year-old new mother and Jason was a 50-year-old new father. Since there had been no period of rest from having babies, gardening, canning, patching, sewing, quilting, etc., Sarah, with the exception of the 1918 influenza attack, seemed to have been in exceptionally good health. Jason chewed tobacco with such great dignity that one never knew for certain that he had a "chow" laying far back in his jaw. Some thought it saved him from that flu. Of course, that was not medical talk, just people talk.

    The Solley children learned early to work hard for what their parents wanted for them and for what they learned to want for themselves. They worked in their own wood-sawing and wood-cutting, cotton fields, pea patches, sorghum cane patches and watermelon patches. They knew how to double-work and go outside the family farm to earn extra money to save. They were taught that this extra work was just a means to a better end. The girls sometimes went to take live-in summer jobs for white families. They cooked, washed, scrubbed floors, etc. The boys went to work outside jobs of yard work and farm work. They were advised to save every possible penny toward more education than Pine Hill Grade School of Plum Creek Valley could offer. They could go farther than that.

Susan

Susan, the first Solley baby, had been going away to school. She had returned with a new sophistication where many things were concerned. She had no less love for Ma and Pa, but she had picked up a new terminology for them, Mother and Daddy. She was letting the younger ones acquire her new way of addressing her parents. She now felt Ma and Pa was old-fashioned and a little "country"-sounding. She now wanted to ask them a question and "test" their thinking as they were so good at doing with all of their children. Susan smiled to herself, as she came into the room where Jason sat reading about Booker T. Washington, the colored educator, and Sarah was writing some letters. Sarah enjoyed writing letters when she could. Susan said, "Mother, Daddy, I want to be a nurse or teach school. Which one do you think would suit me better or I would be better at doing? You must also tell me why you think the way you do. Take as much time as you need to think about this. I'll just sit here and wait."

Sarah and Jason looked at each other and smiled. After a few minutes of thinking, Sarah looked over at Jason first and then to Susan. She said quietly, "Susan, you really care about people, young and old. You would put your whole heart into either being a nurse or a school teacher. You might enjoy being a teacher more. I've noticed you around your younger sisters and brothers. You have always made me feel good because you take so much pains with telling them things to help them. You do try hard and they do listen to you. I say you should strike out for teaching."

Susan felt good that her mother had put so much thought into her response. She smiled at her mother and said, "Thank you so much, Mother." Then she stepped quickly over to hug her mother tight. She now looked across at Daddy Jason who had not been reading his precious book anymore, but listening and smiling.

He then said, "Well, I guess it's Daddy's turn now."

Susan answered, "Yes, Daddy, it's your turn. Come forward with *your* thoughts." Jason started slowly, "Susan, I would be satisfied to see you go in either direction because you demonstrate the ability to really care and you take seriously anything that you have to do. You would be a good nurse or you would be a good school teacher. Take one and run, my girl."

Susan stepped to him, kissed him on the forehead and said, "Thanks, Daddy. I love you both."

Susan Solley set out to further her education in the field of Education because that was what she had started in. That was what she had given her energy and her heart to. She needed more finance than what she had been able to save and what her parents could help her with. The cotton that Jason took to the cotton gin each year from the cotton fields yielded a limited gain towards his children's schooling. Therefore, they could not depend entirely on cotton to help. Besides being able to get into work-study programs for schooling, the children had to apply for scholarships which would supplement all other funds. Susan said to her family after working diligently, "It's good that we Solleys know how to work, and also know that we have to depend on God to strengthen our beliefs as well as our minds and bodies. I *know* that I can make it! I also know that all of us can do whatever we set our minds to."

Her brother John, the fifth brother, said, "Well, Sue, since you are the oldest, it's good to see your determination. It helps the rest of us to believe that we can also follow our dreams. God knew that you needed to be first."

Nona, the second girl was just coming in from milking the cows. She was in good time to put her two cents' worth in. She had set her milk buckets down on the bench near the back door and said, "I missed something, but I heard enough to get in on it. If you two can do what you set your aims on, then I sure can, too. All the rest of the Solleys can, too. I want to be a stenographer. My fingers are very nimble, but also my mind is nimble and quick, too. I would say you need both to be good at being a good secretary or other office helper. That's just what I'm going to be. I keep hearing that it is not so easy for colored girls as it is for white girls to get a job. But since we've been taught to prepare and then go looking, that's just what I'm going to do. When I go looking for that job, I'll be ready to show them that I am the one they should hire to give them the best job possible, regardless if I am a colored girl. I will help them to know that Plum Creek Valley has never put out a better girl for the job."

Nona's Fella

From Pine Hill Grade School to trade school, secretarial school, to music lessons and college the Solley children moved upward. As they got older, they were told to never forget where they had come from. Sarah, always one for adding just one more thought to a seemingly well covered plan, would say to Mindy, or Jim, or Louise, or Gerald, "Never step on *anybody* who is laying in your path. Don't get to where you're going that way. If you have to hurt people to get to your spot, then you don't need to go to your spot. You are setting your eyes on the wrong spot." The children knew that when their mother said those words, she meant business. They should not only listen, but they should remember to do just that.

When Joe Baker became such a loving young man, Sarah included him in her children's "pep rally." He always loved to be included. He was almost like another brother to all of the Solley children except one. That one was Nona, the second girl. When Joe said to Nona one day, "Your mother has always treated me like another son. I look at all the Solley girls like my sisters except you."

Nona smiled and answered, "Why you say that? Am I not good enough to be like your sister, too? I thought I was."

Joe said, "That's not why at all. You too good to be like my sister."

Nona smiled in herself, but said aloud to Joe, "How can I be too good to be like your sister?"

"Just because that's not what I want you to be, like my sister. I want you to let me come to see just you and only you. I would see the others, but they're not the main reason that I would be coming to your house. Now, do you understand?" Joe said very plainly.

Nona was as happy as she could be right now because she had felt this way a long, long time. She was thinking to herself that God sure had taken his long time to answer her prayer. He took not months, but years. Then Nona answered Joe, "I want you to come and see just me, too. I've wanted this long before today."

"I couldn't be any happier that you want what I want," Joe said. Joe didn't know that a long time ago Nona had been the one child to speak up strongly for him because she could see how smart he was and also how really sweet. She had come to his defense and talked against the way he had been treated in Pine Hill Grade School because of his unusually poor English grammar. Nona was 18 and Joe was 19. They didn't have to wait for Nona to get old enough to "take company." That was past the age that Sarah gave her permission for the girls to have a fella. Fifteen was the age when Sarah's ma Mattie gave Sarah permission to "take company." They immediately started to walk and hold hands together, sit in the porch swing together, sit out in the yard under the fig tree together, and so on. They seemed to have just been waiting for those words which each had said the day they expressed themselves. The words were not too early or too late.

The Bakers

    Jennie Baker and Frank Baker had really endeared themselves to the Solley family. Jennie had come to the quilting bees whenever Sarah had invited her. Frank and Jennie had not missed a single one of Jason's speeches at schools or churches. They were just regular people who had needed what the Solleys offered them. They were kind people. They in turn had invited the Solleys to a supper on a Saturday sometimes. Meeting the Bakers turned into a true blessing. The Bakers had made the first move when they had come over after supper a long time ago. They were not the people that some of the Plum Creek Valley inhabitants had made them out to be. They had been clearly misunderstood.
    Sarah and Jason were glad that they had thought of asking the Bakers about helping out when it was hog-killing time. That was always a time when extra hands could be used. They and all the other people in Plum Creek Valley had to take advantage of cold days for their hog-killing. They had no refrigeration. In order to do all of the things required for saving all parts of the hogs for future meat, many hands were needed for fast work. The hogs had been fed good food and fattened for many months. The Bakers had been helping them for several years. It was good plan. Sarah had suggested to Jason, "Why don't we ask Jennie and Frank to help us on hog-kill-

ing days, and we in turn can do something for them. We could swap work just like when I was a girl and had no brothers. My ma, my pa and me used to help with my uncle's farmwork, and my boy cousins would come over and help my pa."

Jason thought for a minute. Then he said, "That sounds like a good idea, my Sarah. What exactly do you have in mind?"

Sarah said quickly, "I could do some sewing for them since Jennie complains that her sewing looks home-made. You could help Frank with his hay-cutting and raking."

Jason often referred to his wife as *my* Sarah when he was feeling very pleased with something she had said or done. Now he thought this was a splendid idea. So, he said, "My Sarah, my Sarah, I think you may have hit the nail right on the head, as the saying goes. I do believe that is a fair-sounding bargain."

It did work out well. Hog-killing time was busy for the Solleys and Bakers. There was meat to cut up for grinding pork sausage, for making head cheese, for making souse, for rending fat to make lye soap, etc. Then there were the hams, shoulders and sides to be cured in the smokehouse. All of that had to be done immediately. There was no time for slowing around. The cold days had to be taken advantage of and fast.

The Bakers knew how to work fast, and they did not mind working. The men killed the hogs and cleaned them out. The women could help to cut and do much of the small pieces of meat. Everybody had to work prodigiously to prepare the meat before it would spoil. When the Bakers would leave for the day, they could take some meat home to put in their pot. Since there was no refrigeration, canning certain parts of the hog was sometimes done. For instance, sausage was not only stuffed and cured in cotton skins, but also fried and canned in Mason-type fruit and vegetable jars. None of the meat was wasted. Even the pig's feet were sometimes pickled. The pork skins that resulted after the fat had been rendered could be used to make delicious crackling cornbread. Since this kind of bread was only seasonal, everybody in the family wanted some whenever it was cooked. It was special.

On hog-killing days there was not only the big black iron wash pot being kept busy in the yard, but smaller pots were simmering on the kitchen stove with the likes of butterbeans, collard greens and some dried fruit. The children who were still young enough to be in Pine Hill Grade School would come home hungry. They would also be very excited because some parts of that fresh hog meat would be seasoned and slowly simmered to make dinner special. Oh, yes, hog-killing days might be extra busy for the grown-ups, but "goody, oh goody" for the youngsters. They loved them.

Nona, Louise, Mindy

President Woodrow Wilson's time was to be greatly remembered where the Solleys were concerned. He was President while they had lived through the devastating influenza epidemic, and just before that was World War I. Although no Solley was eligible to be a soldier, the war still reached its tentacles out and touched them in many ways. It was during Wilson's second term that Sarah had two more babies while the older children were trying to find more education and marriage. Susan had gotten enough college credits to teach in her own Pine Hill Grade School, and she tried hard to be as good a teacher as Miss Jerry Blakeman.

Nona had attended business school for one semester, and she learned to type to a limited degree. She liked it, but she was persuaded to keep her piano lessons going because she could help other colored children. Miriam Kelly, the oldest daughter of the Kelly family that Sarah and her ma Mattie used to wash and iron for, was now a music teacher. She had been giving Nona, Louise and Mindy piano lessons in exchange for their cleaning her house and yard each week. The arrangement was feasible, and it went on for several years. The youngest girls sometimes wanted to complain that they thought it a little unfair for them to walk to town, clean house and yard for three piano lessons each week. Sarah and Jason had to remind them of something.

Jason called the three girls in and said quietly, "Your mother and I can see that you girls, Nona, Louise, Mindy, are doing very well with your piano lessons. Mindy, first, tell us why you believe you are doing fine with your music?"

Mindy said quickly, "Because I like it!"

Jason replied, "All right. Now, Louise, why are your piano lessons sounding good to you?"

Louise said, smartly, she thought, "I not only like it, but I practice, practice and practice just the way our piano teacher says we have to do."

Nona, oldest of the three sisters, Jason had left for last. He said, "Nona, what's your feelings about those piano lessons?"

Nona had started taking lessons when she was about nine. She was really playing well. So she answered. "Daddy, I like it. I also practice a whole lot, but if Miss Miriam had not given her old piano to us, none of us would be doing so good. We would not have our own piano to practice all those hours on."

Now, Jason had liked all of the answers his three daughters had given. Nona's answer included exactly the sentence he was hoping to hear. So Jason looked over to Sarah and smiled. The girls looked from one parent to the other.

Then Sarah sat up tall in her rocking chair, looked back at Jason. Then looking from one girl to the other, she said, "Having a piano to practice what you learn from your teacher is the one thing that you needed as much as the lessons. Your teacher who remembered all the pretty washed, starched and ironed dresses, aprons, shirts and pants that your Grandma Mattie and your mother Sarah used to do for her family every week. We did up a whole lot of clothes. She is a good woman, and she has not forgotten. Life is a whole lot of doing good for one another on this earth." Sarah looked again toward Jason after she had finished talking to the girls.

Jason knew she expected more from him. He said, "One day you girls will listen to yourselves playing for yourselves, your children, your churches, schools and whatever. Then you'll know that getting all of this from a little work is worth all. So, let's not have any more complaining. Be thankful that you can walk to town, you can work for your piano lessons, and you can come home and practice on your very own piano, which was a gift. Let's not hear anymore because when you are complaining God is not smiling. The girls said almost in a chorus to their mother and their daddy, "Thank you." They were doing their teaching.

From that day on, nothing but good things was spoken about those precious piano lessons. Nona was glad that she knew how to use the typewriter. She now had one of her very own, but she was most happy that her piano teacher had said, "Nona, you now know enough about the piano and music to start classes for many girls and boys in the Plum Creek Valley area and also in other areas of the deep South. You should consider being a music teacher. You have so much talent. You also know how to stick to what you really believe in. I do like the way you commit. I will help you and I will guide your steps if you won't throw your talent away. Do think about this."

Nona was happy to see that her teacher had so much faith in her. She answered, "Miss Miriam, you have made me so happy. I shall tell Mother and Daddy. I am also going to talk to my beau. He's been my beau a long time even before he knew he was my beau. I've been his girl even longer than that. We are gonna get married."

Miriam said, "Nona, pray tell me what in the world do you mean? When you say you've been his girl longer than that, what exactly does that mean? I really do think I have an idea, but I want to hear you explain it." Miriam was smiling as she talked. She knew exactly what Nona was talking about.

Nona said, "Well, it's like this. I liked him when I first met him even though he was different from my brothers or the other boys I'd seen. He talked different. His family was not from Plum Creek Valley. Though he was different, I sensed it was not his fault. He was sort of pushed aside, but I could see his heart. It was good, and he was trying to hide it so he wouldn't get hurt by people who thought they were better than he was. My mother first became his friend, she thought, but I was already his friend in my heart. He is sweet and he is smart."

Joe did well in Pine Hill School. Then he went "off to school." He made good use of his time and talents. He became a grade school teacher. At that time many colored grade school teachers just had to be smart and have a certain amount of credits (preferably college, but not necessarily). They had to continue going to Saturday classes or summer school. Some of them made excellent teachers. They gave a lot extra when they taught these children because they really saw and felt the need. Joe was one of these very, very devoted teachers. He worked hard to keep himself qualified and all the children satisfied. Word was out that children learned when Joe Baker was their teacher. Joe Baker loved for his school children to make progress.

Joe said to his ma and pa, Jenny and Frank Baker, "It is time for me to ask the prettiest and sweetest girl in, not only Plum Creek Valley, but in all of the deep South, to marry me. You already know that it is Nona. I love that girl so much."

Joe's ma said, "Oh, thank the Lord! You can't ever ever do no better. You keep on loving her now! Never stop loving that girl. Don't you ever stop!" With those words, Jennie hugged her son.

Frank Baker stood smiling as wide as he could smile. Then he said, "Boy, you sho' do know how to pick a wife. She a fine girl. But I better wait to see if she gonna pick you back." Then Frank laughed heartily. After that, he patted his Joe hard on the back. Joe left laughing and saying, "I'm on my way to ask her. Pray that she accepts me."

They said in unison, "You know we gonna do it!"

Nona accepted Joe's marriage proposal which she already knew was coming soon. They were surely ready for each other. They were surely ready for each other. When they told Nona's mother Sarah and her daddy Jason, neither of them were surprised. They had seen it coming. These two had reminded them so much of themselves when they were that age. Nona was 19, but Joe was just 20. They had been saving their money. If they remembered to be careful, they would be just fine. They bought a little bungalow house. They married at Nona's and Joe's church. The wedding was beautiful, and the new couple rode off in Joe's buggy to their home. Both of them kept right on with their music and teaching. One day God would give them a nice baby boy or baby girl. Until then they would just keep loving each other and Nona would keep working. The year was 1920.

Jim

Jim, the oldest of the Solley boys, had finished Pine Hill School and went off to Pittsburgh, Pennsylvania, to seek a railroad job. The Solleys didn't live too far from a railroad. Jim had always been so fascinated by trains. When he was a little boy, he had said, "When I get big, I'm gonna learn how to drive a train. Then I'll ride the train every day." He had said to Daddy Solley that he was gonna make a whole lot of money working on the train. One day he said without warning, "Pa, where is Ma?"

Jason said, "I think she is in the smokehouse. Why?"

Jim said, "I want to go get her so I can hug her and hug you, too, because I'm gonna go to get me a job on a train." Jim did not wait for a reply, but went straight to the smokehouse where his mother Sarah was cutting off meat for dinner. He started right out with, "Ma, I love you and Pa. Both of you are so good to all of us children. We are real lucky to have two such people to be our ma and pa. I been wanting to work on a train ever since I got tired of plowing, picking cotton and cutting cane. Well, I guess it started longer ago than that. When I used to see the men on the train, I would wish that it could be me. I knew I was not gonna be picking, plowing and cutting stalks the rest of my life. I'm gonna go to Pittsburg. Rev. Clark said that he would give me a letter of reference. He said he will never forget this family's goodness and faithfulness. I will catch a train with some of the money I have saved. I'm gonna go tomorrow. I can't wait no longer."

Sarah looked at her oldest son, and then she looked at Jason. Jason did the same. He looked at Jim and he looked at Sarah. They saw the determination in Jim. Both reached out to him, and they all three were hugging each other. They wished for him God's blessings. The others who were home were called to wish their oldest brother well. Jim promised to stay in touch often. He also said he felt sure he'd get a job on the train. He was happy. He said further that when things started going well with him, he would see what some of his younger brothers might be able to do on the train. He would not forget them.

Sarah packed Jim's grip, and the next day they drove into town for Jim to catch the train. As Jim waved out of the window, the family present said prayers for him.

Hazel, Ray, Gerald, Charley, and Jim Crow Laws

Hazel, the fifth Solley girl, was called by some of the Solley family members "The Dreamer" because she often expressed her private desires aloud after a time. She loved to read. Her reading often reminded Sarah of Jason, except Hazel read more fantasy than her daddy. This did not mean she skipped over the factual literature, because she certainly did not. Hazel read history books because she never seemed to tire of learning about life in this and other countries. She liked being able to see how far colored people had come since they started coming to this country before the Mayflower. She read and then she visualized what colored people might be doing by the end of the 19th century. She thought about going to other places that were not in the deep South, but were still in these United States of America. She thought about Sojourner Truth, the slave woman who found ways through the Underground Railroad to lead many slaves to the North and into freedom because she was smart, and she wanted to see her people free.

Hazel even dreamed about going to faraway places. One day she said to Sarah, "Ma, I'm going to Africa, and I'll see where we came from. Maybe I can figure out why we were picked out of that country and brought to this country to work as slaves."

Sarah replied, "That sounds just like you, my girl Hazel. You do like to get to the bottom of things. Maybe you'll be able to open many eyes, and maybe the understanding will somehow bring about more satisfaction for colored people. Right now, though, we should think hard every day about how to go from where we are to where we think we should be." Hazel agreed that she meant to do just that. too.

Ray loved to make things almost as much as his brother Gerald. Although Ray was two years older than Gerald, he could not quite keep up with Gerald's ability to build little wagons, tree swings, play houses, etc. He was. therefore, just a bit jealous and a little vindictive at times. Their daddy Jason noticed this and decided that he had to address this situation. One day he called the two boys and said this: "I've noticed that both you boys enjoy making things around the barnyard. I also see that you have different talents. Some things, Ray, you can make easier and quicker than Gerald. Some things, Gerald, you are more adept at than Ray. Both of you are good with what the Good Lord gave you. Do you agree?"

Gerald said, "I try to do the best I can with making a little wagon or whatever, but Ray gets mad because he says I'm trying to do better than he does. I don't try to do that. I just do it the best way I see how to do it. Is that wrong, Pa?"

Jason said, "I'm going to ask Ray that questions. Ray, what do you think? Be very honest now."

Ray answered slowly, "I don't know what he's talking about when he says that I get mad. I guess I don't like it when his stuff always looks so perfect. I guess I do get mad with myself because he can do better. I don't really get that mad. I get disgusted with me, though."

Jason said, "Well, Ray, what do you think you ought to do about this way you feel about your brother?"

Ray answered, "Gerald, I'm sorry for acting ugly with you. Maybe I should find something I can do real good. I'm sure there is some other thing that will make me feel I can do good, too."

Gerald answered, "It's all right, Ray. I know lots of things you can do real good. We can both do whatever makes us feel the best. I'm sure God didn't mean for everybody to do everything good. We all got something. Let's do what we can do . Then we can still be good brothers. Ain't that right, Pa?"

Jason had been sitting, and now he stood up, smiling happily, and said, "I am glad that my two boys have solved this little problem. I did not do it. You two did it yourselves. Now isn't that just so nice?"

Ray spoke first and said, "Pa, I'm glad you made us talk. I like Gerald better now because nothing was his fault. It was my fault for feeling the way I did." He went to his brother and patted him on the shoulder. Now everything was all right. From that day on, Ray stopped trying to compete with his younger brother and put his mind to things he could enjoy more.

When Jason had shared this with Sarah, she had smiled and said, "You know so well how to solve the children's problems by letting them do it themselves, which is really much better anyway."

Charley Solley did enjoy going to school because learning new facts was his passion. Going to a one-room school for Charley meant that he took full advantage of listening to assignment reports from school children in classes above him. All of the classes could at some time or other have a chance to do this. Sometimes the teacher would combine classes. For instance, a third and fourth grade class might do the same spelling lessons or the same arithmetic lessons. This meant one class instead of two. Geography class might be taught to fifth and sixth graders at the same time. This was one way that the teacher could cover the classes. Charley would go home from school and share with Sarah some of what he learned in geography and physiology. It didn't matter if she was cooking or patching overworn clothes, Charley would burst right in spewing out his information. He's say, "Guess what I found out today, the *Petrified Forest* have tree logs that were turned to stone or the *Grand Canyon* is a place I just got to go to see when I grow up. I got to see the *Grand Canyon!*"

Sarah, always one to sound interested, would say, "Why, Charley, I do believe you will one day go to see this place. Maybe you'll come back and take your pa and ma to see it, too. We'd like that."

Charley would say, "Oh, yeah, Ma, by that time I'll have a job making more money than Pa does and making more money than you make when you go to town peddling."

Sarah did seem to enjoy her early morning trips to town in the buggy to peddle her fresh garden vegetables and fruit. Sometimes she'd take a few dozen eggs. If it was not a school day, sometimes she'd take one of the children. Charley always was anxious to go. He knew he could bend his ma's ears about all the things he wanted to do and all the places he wanted to go after he finished school. He saw himself with a job like a white man.

Sarah would rise a little earlier on the day she was going to town. She always hoped to sell her produce and return home before it got so hot. Sarah would knock on back doors until she got responses. She had some regular customers, and she looked out for new customers. Some didn't mind paying 15 cents a gallon for fresh Kentucky Wonder green beans. Others were trying to get Sarah to sell for ten cents a gallon.

Sometimes when Sarah had sold all of her wares, she would take her newly earned money into some of the stores to buy needed things to take home. Whenever she had one of the children with her, she was really careful to observe all of the *Jim Crow Laws*. Oh yes, since 1890 there were many laws for whites and laws for coloreds. Water fountains were often clearly marked. Public toilets and other facilities were, too. Jason always believed in respecting laws, even though he knew they were not always what he and Sarah thought were fair.

One day as Sarah and Charley were driving home from a peddling trip and Charley was enjoying his bottle of soda water, he felt good enough to ask his ma a question that was troubling him. He said, "Ma, can you help me understand why we have to drink out of different places and go the toilet in different places 'cause we colored? We always clean because you and Pa see to that. We don't throw paper and trash on the ground or on the floor. You and Pa told us these things ever since we were born."

Now, Sarah wished for Jason to help her give Charley the right answer. She wanted to give a fair answer. She wanted Charley to know that these laws did not mean that white people hated colored people. She wanted him to know that some white people liked some colored people as well as they did some other white people. Oh, how she wished for her Jason right now. He would be able to say just the very words that were necessary. Well, Jason was home and working in the field.

Sarah answered Charley's question, "Charley, you have asked your ma a question. She wants to give you the right answer as best she can. We colored people do what we do because it is the law. Somebody in the law decided that coloreds and whites are not equal enough to share. It don't mean they think we dirty or poison, though. It may sound like it, but it don't mean that at all. Maybe one day you or some other coloreds can help change bad laws."

Charley had listened very carefully to every word Sarah said. He tried not to miss what she explained. Then he thought and thought. He liked the way Sarah had explained it. She always made things so plain, but he still did not quite understand. He still did not quite like it. Then he said, "I sho' did like the nice way you talked. You made it plain as you could. I just still don't think it is right. Do you think it is right, Ma?"

Sarah had to give her boy an honest answer. Sarah said, "Well, I really don't think it's right because it makes us feel like we not quite good enough. Some of us might not do just right about everything, but some of them don't do just right either. Remember what I said, Charley?"

"What you mean, Ma?" Charley asked.

"I said maybe one day you may be one of the people to help to change bad laws."

Charley had been sitting with his head down. Now, he raised it up with new determination. He blurted out loud, "Yeah, Ma, I expect I just might be one to help get that bad law changed. I'm sho' gonna be keeping that in my mind."

Charley and Sarah rode and looked out on the fields of green corn, sugar cane and black-eyed peas. They would soon be home. Some of the children would go to the plum thickets later.

Sarah and Nona and Babies

Sarah and Jason were expecting their 12th little Solley baby. It was a very special time for the Solley family because Nona, the second child, and her husband Joe Baker had just had their first child. This child of Nona and Joe would be the first child of the fourth generation of slave-born foreparents. There was Lawrence and Mattie, the parents of Sarah; Sarah and Jason, the parents of Nona; Nona and Joe, the parents of Joe Jr. who was born March 20, 1921. Little Sophie came along July 11, 1921.

Nona came into her mother's room and held little Joe up to little Sophie and said to her baby boy, "Little Joe, meet your very newest little aunt, Sophie."

Sarah sat up on her pillow and looking down at little Sophie said, "Now meet your first little nephew."

Everybody laughed happily. Joe and Jason just reached out and shook each other's hand. Nona went closer to her mother in the bed and reached down to kiss her and her new little sister. The two men could not let this opportunity pass to show how much they appreciated and loved their wives. Jason could not resist this little piece of fatherly advice to his son-in-law, "Joe, son, when things between you and Nona are not in perfect agreement, remember that this may be your best time to grow closer. But you'll only grow closer if you listen to each other. Then after listening to each other, try to really hear each other. This may sound like double talk, but let me warn you it is not at all. You cannot hear each other if you are too busy hearing your own selves. Does that make sense?"

"I have always found you to be so wise and so fair. I am thinking about what you have just said. I am trying honestly to understand exactly what you mean by listening and hearing. On the surface they sound like the same thing, but knowing how you think, Mr. Solley, I know they're not all the same thing," Joe said.

"You are so right, my son. Let us see what my wise wife Sarah has to say that might explain what I mean. Believe me, we have had lots of practice at this," answered Jason.

Sarah and Nona had stopped looking at the babies and at each other. They were listening to the two men. They found the conversation fascinating and also a bit exhilarating.

Sarah commented, "Jason is saying that we have to not believe our own way of thinking is the right way all the time. We have to give the other one a little credit for having a little sense, too. We can't believe that our way is always the best way and the way that we should go. Sho' 'nuf trouble is going to come when one does not want to give the other one any credit for having any sense. If you looking for trouble, you sho' gonna find it this way. You gonna find a heap o' trouble. Fix it before it fixes you both."

Joe said, "Well, if I can't understand that, I can't understand anything. I should stop thinking I can teach school children anything at all." With that said, Joe laughed heartily.

It was now Nona's time to add or subtract a few words. She held her little son close to her breast. She kissed him several times. Then she looked around at everybody one at a time, then said, "Always leave it to my mother to sum it all up in such a way that my littlest piano lesson child can understand. I just hope that the Good Lord gives me that kind of good sense. I hope that he also gives me Mama Jennie Baker's good kind heart to add to what I got from my parents. This little fella that I'm holding will then be a blessed child. If we have more babies, they will be blessed, too. I have a good man for my husband. If he gets the wisdom of my daddy and the sweetness of his daddy, we will not only just listen to each other, but we'll hear each other. Then our children will reap the blessing." Nona finished this feeling pretty good.

Visiting time must close for the Bakers and the Solleys. Nona had two piano lessons to give in an hour. The baby would go down for his nap, and Joe would fry the fish, cook the corn and green Kentucky Wonder beans for their evening meal. Nona liked it when Joe cooked. He could beat her cooking so many things. She would churn the milk and put the butter away. She hoped Joe would make his special little turnover corn bread patties today. She loved to put butter on it.

Sarah was lying in her confinement bed. The little new girl was not six weeks old. That, of course, meant that Sarah had long ago been taught how to obey the rules for after a new baby came. All of the children who were still at home and big enough to help Jason helped. Those were old rules. They were rules that didn't have to be written anywhere. Everybody learned them as they got bigger and bigger. Sarah had to take care of herself for them. Jason said if they all took good care of her she would be able to do just that.

Fishing

Every time Jason caught up with the work that must be done around the house and barn and field, he would go fishing, even if for a very short time. At times Plum Creek could really get busy. People in Plum Creek Valley area thought they were the luckiest people in the deep South, and some thought, even in the United States of America. Fishing was considered just that good. They would catch grinners, catfish, white perch, etc. Almost everybody loved fish. Even the ones who had gotten fish bone scares. This meant that some fish was good, but bony. The small bones sometimes got stuck in a throat here and there, especially if people were fish hungry and ate fast. There was one thing though, you never heard of anyone dying because a fish bone stuck in the throat. They ate cornbread crust and drank buttermilk to push the bone out of the throat. Everybody knew that much.

When Jason took the children fishing, it was so much more than recreation. Besides recreation, it was a time to supplement the hog meat and the chicken on the table. Hog meat had to last a long, long time. Therefore, only a limited amount could be eaten each day. Chickens were a second source of meat, but even that had to be somewhat limited. Fish was good. Sarah would often remind the family. She would say, "Now we can't eat eggs every day for breakfast."

Somebody would say, "Why, Ma? Don't we have a whole lot o' eggs?"

Sarah would say, "They may look like a whole lot, but don't forget that I have to take eggs to town to peddle. Don't you ever forget that now!"

Some young child would sometimes ask, "Ma, why you have to put our eggs and our roasting ears of corn and our peaches in the basket to take to the people in town so much? Why don't they grow theirs?"

Sarah thought sometimes that she would never stop having to answer this question. She would patiently and carefully say, "We need the extra money to buy the things that we cannot grow in our garden and in our fields." She would sometimes add, " We still have some left for us. We don't peddle it all away."

When Jason would take the children fishing, this was a good time to do some more teaching about many things. Jason did not let many opportunities pass for telling his children things that would help them live better. He always figured they would need all the help he and Sarah together could give them. He told them again and again how important it was for them to be prepared to take advantage of the 15th Amendment and always vote as soon as they became old enough to be eligible. The children heard this over and over again. He explained at every chance he had the meaning and the consequences of the *Jim Crow Laws* in their place of living. Jason tried as hard as Sarah to help all of their children understand how important it was for them to keep trying to improve their living status by preparing themselves with college or a trade. He would say to them, "If you find yourself not knowing what you want to do with your life, just stop right there! Say out loud the things you believe you don't want to do. That should help you make a decision."

The children looked forward to going on these fishing trips. They found never a dull moment. While Jason was doing his teaching, the children never had to stop fishing to listen. They learned to bait their hooks with healthy-looking earth worms that they dug from the back yard or behind the smokehouse.

One disadvantage of fishing in different parts of Plum Creek was mosquitoes. Some areas of good biting by the fish were also areas of good biting by those hated little flying insects. Jason or Sarah would remind the children to go to the old rag box kept in one of the cribs and bring some rags to burn very slowly in the shady swampy area of the creek. The mosquitoes hated this old rag smoke. They would fly away fast. The family could fish in peace.

One day John and Mark, who were only two years apart in their ages, were responsible for going to the crib in the barn to get the rags. They decided, as they often did, to play a trick on the fishing group. They did not consider that the trick would also include them. They pretended to get the rags and didn't really get them. When the fishing party got into the deep dark area of Plum Creek where the fish loved to bite the worms on the hooks, and where the biting insects were hiding, Jason said, "Now, let's hurry and start our smoking rags."

John said, "Mark, don't you have them?"

Mark quickly answered, "John, I thought you had them."

Jason said, "Well, it looks like we can't let our little insects eat us all up today. What do you say, Mark, and what do you say, John?" Jason knew exactly what to do.

John said, "Maybe we can all get in the wagon and go to town and carry our picnic basket for a town picnic."

Jason said, "I have a better idea. Everybody who went

fishing besides John and Mark will go back for the rags. This time we'll smoke away the mosquitoes and have a good time catching lots of fish. Mark and John will stay home and work new arithmetic problems and learn new spelling words to report to me later."

The young Solley boys had plenty to keep them busy while the other members of the family fished and smoked the mosquitoes away. When the family returned home with lots of fish to be scaled, the two little spoil-sport boys had to get busy cleaning fish. Then they had to give a full report of their assignment while the fish was frying. The two young Solley boys discovered that playing a cruel trick at the expense of others does not pay off. It was not all funny, they discovered.

Jason said after supper, "Did everybody enjoy your afternoon?"

Everybody chorused, "Yes, yes!" Everybody except John and Mark had answered.

Jason said, "I am sure John and Mark just wanted to have a little fun, but fun should not put others at a disadvantage. At least, some more spelling words and arithmetic problems were learned. So it was not a complete lost."

Jason and Sarah did not consider themselves mean parents because they sometimes had to exercise strict rules. They felt strongly that God must have a good reason for giving them this big charge to keep. They never resented it. Both just believed strongly that they should please God by doing their best. Sarah now remembered a prayer she had sent up to heaven when Jason was her fella. He was the fella she wanted and the Good Lord had given her Jason. Now, she enjoyed the things that made their life so right. She still does not think she is a good cook

Using the Land

Even though the area of Plum Creek Valley that the Solleys lived in was pretty fertile, Jason still had to sometimes use a limited amount of fertilizer for his crops. They saved all of the manure that was cleaned up around the barnyard to put on watermelon patches, greens patches, cantaloupe patches, etc. Sarah treasured her huge garden and used animal manure often for it, too. However, Jason had to get to town and buy some commercial fertilizer sometimes. This took cash. Jason had heard that some white men could go and get it on credit, and then pay for it when the crops were finished. He tried hard to use as little as he could get by with, and pay as he bought. His watermelons were said to be the best in Arkansas. But, of course, he always said that it really depended on who said it. It still pleased him that his melons were recognized and highly praised. All of the Solley children had always enjoyed their own watermelons.

    Sarah's two pear trees produced for Sarah the most delicious pears. Sarah knew how to make the best pear preserves. That was one thing that Sarah refused to sell for money in town. Her family loved them too well. They took the place of syrup with buttered biscuits for breakfast. They also took the place of plum and peach cobblers for dinner and supper. They made a very special addition for any meal. So Sarah made up her mind really early that these would be for her own family most of the time. The only time that Sarah shared these was with someone who was sick. She had such a good heart for sick people. She never tired of sick people. You could hear her calling, "Gerald or John or Ray (if a man was sick), I want you to take this jar of pear preserves and some mustard greens to the sick."

The boy would answer, "Ma, do you want me to go right now?"

"Yes, I want you to go right now so it will be in plenty of time before they feed him his dinner."

"All right, Ma, I'm coming right away."

If a woman was sick, Sarah would call not one girl, but always two girls. She might call, "Louise, come to the kitchen. Where's Mindy? Tell her to come, too."

"All right, Ma, I get her," Louise would say. The girls did not have to ask why Sarah called one boy for such a sick trip, but always two girls. They knew it was an unwritten rule that the Solley girls went places in pairs. A long time ago it was asked, "Ma, why do I have to stop my embroidering to go, too?"

Sarah had made it very plain and clear, "Two girls go together from this house so they can protect each other. If some boy or dirty man see a girl going through the wooded path or down the railroad track by herself, then he might get ugly ideas in his ugly head. If he sees two of you going together, then he know to keep a'going where he started." All of the Solley girls got the meaning. They all knew that when their mother talked like this to listen big.

NAACP

In 1909 the National Association for the Advancement of Colored People was formed. The Solleys wanted to be sure to learn all they could about this great new organization for theirs and their children's advancement. They knew that from all they heard and could read about this NAACP that it would be a saving grace in many places for colored people. Jason and Sarah would sit down and talk to their children about how this new great organization could help them. They wanted to allow their lives to be affected and their children's children.

When Jason had an opportunity to include the NAACP in any of his public talks about the better future of the colored people, he did not hesitate to do it. He would often say that, "My speeches are not to entertain or to give you another chance to leave the house. I hope they encourage and enlighten you so that you can begin to see how to make more progress than we have seen since the signing of the Emancipation Proclamation in 1863."

Somebody in the church or school house would raise a hand and say, "Mr. Solley, what can I do down here in Plum Creek Valley to help us?"

Jason Solley would answer by asking another question. He'd say, "Can anybody here tonight tell us what we can do to make our freedom more meaningful?"

Sometimes a brave woman would raise her hand to say, "We can find out how to be a member of this NAACP. Then they can lead us into what we need to do. They have to be able to help so we can help."

Jason would be pleased for that kind of thinking. He would say strongly, "Now, there's a start for us if anybody agrees." At this, hands would go up in agreement all over the room. Now Jason would be pleased that his crowd had some willing participants. He could not let the new interest die here. He promised to do some fact-finding and to help his audience get involved. Jason was a man of his word. He got busy and Plum Creek Valley had many participants in this wonderful new organization that would fight for their rights.

The Bakers, Jennie and Frank, were finding out more than they had dreamed they would ever know. They knew that when their boy Joe had become a friend of the Solleys it was the beginning of a new life in Plum Creek Valley for the three of them. This speech that Jason made lifted them up after this latest program, and they went home feeling like Plum Creek Valley was truly home. They were no more outsiders.

After Jason's speech was finished and people were scattering to go home, Sarah went to Jason and said, "Mr. Jason, oh, my Jason, what in the world would I ever do without you?"

He turned to look at this little wife and smiled. He was a tall man, but he even looked taller to her at this moment. He said, "That is something we hope you won't have to do for a long time. With that, she linked her arm in his free arm and they walked happily to their wagon.

Madam C.J. Walker's Hair Care

During the night the rain had ceased. The sun was now just peeping up above the horizon. It was surely going to be a nice day. It was going to be nice for a lot of reasons. Sarah was going to make her daily Bible reading a little longer. She was going to make a special breakfast just for Jason and herself. Jason had left the house and had gone out to the barn to feed some stock and to let some others out to pasture and pond. Claude, Edward and Sophie had gone to Texarkana, Texas, to visit their Aunt Pearl for a week. Visits like this were rare, but they were also precious. Money had to be carefully saved for the train ride and maybe some new shoes.

The children always went barefoot in warm weather until Sunday. This would keep the shoes from wearing out too fast. Of course, the children grew fast. So there was always the watch out for not letting shoes wait for Sunday too much. Then they could become outgrown and really pinch the feet. So when shoes and clothes were passed down to the next brother or sister, it was a big help. It was just a must!

Sometimes though the younger child would ask, "Ma, when am I gonna get some brand new shoes?"

Sarah would answer, "Maybe when you wear these out. Maybe then there won't be any to pass down to you at that time."

The answer from the complaining child might be, "I hope I get to be the one first to wear the new shoes next time."

Sarah would first smile to the child, then say, "Maybe so." Since Claude and Edward were only one year apart and were the two baby boys as well as the two babies of the whole family, they sometimes could not pass down their clothes. They were often so near the same size until many people who didn't know them thought they were twins. These two boys liked each other so much until it would please them to be looking like each other. That is, most of the time.

When Sarah had finished her Bible reading, wiped her reading spectacles again, she yawned pleasantly, and got up go to the kitchen. She went to the canning jar shelves in the pantry end of the long kitchen to get something special. She took down a quart jar of sage and red paper sausage. The canned sausage made at hog-killing time were always put on a high shelf because the family only ate this for really special occasions. It was unlike the smoked meat kept out in the smokehouse hanging and dripping a little down on pure tin troughs. The tin was to protect and prevent accidental fires in the smokehouse. Sarah put the pre-fried sausage in an iron skillet to heat in the oven. She made some of her beautiful white fluffy biscuits, opened a jar of her pear preserves, scrambled fresh eggs while the coffee was perking. Then she went to the window to see if Jason had started in from the barnyard. She didn't see him yet. She set the table. He should be coming by now, she was thinking. Just as she said to herself, "I'd better go get my Jason. He's trying to finish something." She heard him kick his shoes against the steps. She hurried to the kitchen door and greeted him with "Hi, there, Mr. Jason Solley! Your wife has made breakfast. I hoped you'd get here before I had to come get you."

Jason smelled the food before he was halfway to the house. He grabbed his Sarah, pulled her to him and said, "You know I can hardly wait for you and breakfast. I've washed my hands already in our crib wash house." With that, said Jason sat at the head of the table. This was his place all the years of their marriage. Her place was at the other end. The family called it the foot of the eating table. They were both hungry, but would not think of beginning to eat until the food had been blessed and they had given God thanks.

As the two older Solleys ate their delicious breakfast, they enjoyed each other's conversation. Since Jason did not have anything pressing on him to do today, he had been persuaded by his Sarah to catch the train and go to Kirksville with Sarah to get her hair dressed. This was an occasional trip for Sarah. Usually she did everything necessary to her hair herself. Now that her reading had introduced her to Madam C.J. Walker's hair care, she could not rest until she got herself some of the products and got her hair dressed. She knew that this was maybe a little bit waste, but it was the one thing that interested her besides Jason and the children. It was some years before she did anything about what she had been reading. Now she was most pleased to save her peddling money for something that was just for her. She felt extremely lifted when she took this train trip. Jason had convinced her that if any woman in America, colored or white, deserved this special treat, it was his Sarah. He knew just how to make her feel so special still. After 14 children, Sarah still felt very special.

When it was possible for Jason to go with her, he really did enjoy himself. He would use a little of his watermelon, cantaloupe, tomato patch and firewood savings to go. While Sarah got her Madam C.J. Walker hair fixings, Jason looked around town and read something that he'd bought in town.

They could have brought a snack of crispy fried chicken from home, but they decided against this. The older children would have reprimanded them kindly by saying, "Oh, Mother, do you have to fix a lunch for a trip like this for you and Daddy? Make this a really fun trip. I've been working enough to help buy your snack for today." This kind of talk would be enough to convince Sarah to just sit on the train and enjoy the trip. She would smile to herself as the train sped down the railroad track, and she would think how it did not take much to convince her to leave that chicken in the coop.

As the train moved very fast, it seemed that the barns, houses, cows and beautiful flowers beside the track got out of sight too fast. There were oaks, pine and sweet gum trees that seemed to meet them and leave them so quickly. Some of the flowers were wild and others were in people's yards or gardens. Sarah loved all the flowers. These reminded her of her own yard. Jason's eyes fell on the laid-by crops along the railroad. He reached over from time to time and patted Sarah on her hands clutching her white pocketbook laying in her lap. She was extra pleased that she could finally take time and money to give herself this pleasant trip.

It was a pleasure trip in more than one way. She closed her eyes to think and let her imagination run wild. She could only keep them closed the shortest time. There was too much to see along the way. The train carried them past one yard which reminded both Jason and Sarah of their own yard back at home. The wisteria growing on a trellis over a brick walkway from the front gate to the steps looked almost like home. Sarah and Jason looked straight at one another at the very same instant. They were thinking the same thing. They had a childish thought that was, "Oh, how pretty! But it is not as pretty as ours in our yard though!"

They finally reached Kirksville for the second part of their venture. They stepped down from the train onto the little metal step-down by the conductor who made sure that Sarah did not fall. As Sarah's feet touched the ground, she felt as light and happy as if she was about "Sweet Fifteen" all over again.

They could walk from the train station to the part of town that housed the Madam C.J. Walker's Shop. It was just long enough for an enjoyable walk. They had a little extra time before Sarah's appointment, and they did a little window shopping. The first thing of interest to Sarah was man's suit in the window. Oh, how she wished she could get that suit for her Jason. All the years he had worked and helped his children grow up, and had helped them go to school, and had helped them with their mathematics, etc. had not earned him a full suit like the one she was looking at in that store window. Yes, her Jason always wore a white shirt that had been starched and ironed by her or one of the girls, with his black Sunday pants and jacket. But it was not a full suit like the one in the store window. Oh, how she wished he could have a suit like that when he went to his Masonic Lodge's grand meetings once a year. Sure, she would like to see him in it every Sunday, too. She would like to see him in it when he was standing up speaking to colored people about different subjects and saying speeches that would help them enjoy life after slavery. She thought so hard about this. Her mind was racing fast. She said out loud, "Jason, just look at that full suit! You sho' would look good in that when you go dressed up! Ain't that a pretty suit?"

Jason had noticed how wide Sarah's eyes had been getting as she stepped from one side to the other of that suit in the window. It was a black pin stripe. Well, he knew he had to answer his Sarah and quick, too. He smiled at her and said,

"Yes, my Sarah, that is a real nice suit. It is pretty, too. I'd be real dressed up in that. The problem is, I can't afford to buy it. Now can I?"

Sarah came right back at her husband with, "Maybe you can't afford to buy it, but somebody can!"

Jason said, "What in God's green earth are you talking about, my Sarah?"

Sarah smiled, "Listen to me, and I tell you exactly what I'm talking about. You got 14 children, and all but three are no longer home most of the time. They are married or working or going to school part-time and working full-time. They sho' can buy their nice daddy a suit so he won't have to wear a mismatched suit no more."

Jason said, "How do you see fixing that?"

Sarah answered her husband quickly, "Leave it to me. Just don't you worry one hair off your head."

Jason said, "I won't say another word, my Sarah." Sarah disappeared into the store after she had said, "Wait here a minute."

Jason stood watching the people on the street until Sarah returned with the needed information in her white pocketbook. She caught Jason's hand and said, "Let's go to Madam C.J. Walker's hair dressing place. Your Sarah got to get herself all pretty for you today."

Jason looked at Sarah and smiled. They kept walking. Sarah let go of Jason's arm. She was in good time. He left her to her hair dressing and walked down the street. He would see what he could, and maybe buy a newspaper or magazine. Then he'd come back to get his wife so that they could go "good eating." Then they would catch the train and get back to their home before dark. That was just what they did.

The hair dressing place was so pretty inside. Sarah always felt good. She would think to herself that their house in Plum Creek Valley should look so good as this. She knew that this fine stuff must have cost a whole lot of money. She would keep her home pretty as she could.

Ray, Charley, John, Mark and Hazel

Sarah and Jason arrived home in time to take care of the outside of their house. Jason fed and put the farm animals in their stalls. Sarah milked the cows and strained the milk. Then she went to the hen house to gather the eggs. No cooking supper was needed. They were full of their Kirksville meal, and they could just make the best of their evening. Sarah did not start any sewing or quilt piecing. Jason did not start any reading, writing or studying. They put a perfect end to their wonderful day by just enjoying each other's company and retiring early. Jason could not resist touching Sarah.

Jason looked at the reflection of himself and his Sarah in their dresser mirror. He gave thanks quietly to God for their blessings of life, love and children. He could think of no other woman that he had ever known before or after his marriage to Sarah that he would have remotely considered for his wife. Yes, Sarah had been born to be his wife. He had been born to be her husband. They prayed for all of their children who were leading their different lives. Jim did get a job with the Pennsylvania railroad. Ray and Charley also had jobs with Jim's company. So Jim did well and did not forget his family. Susan married her college beau, and they and their three children resided in Little Rock, Arkansas. John and Mark joined their talents in carpentry. They built together. It was said of them, "If you need any thing built, go to the Solley Brothers' Shop." Hazel, "The Dreamer" became a singer and showgirl. She went first to New York City, and then got an offer to go to Paris, France. That offer to work in Paris was a part of Hazel's dream of going to faraway places. She had promised Sarah and Jason a trip to Paris after she saved a little more. Hazel could think of nothing to please herself more. She was a very determined girl, and she dearly loved her ma and pa. It seemed like Gerald took a while to find out exactly what it was that he wanted to do. Even though he had shown a lot of talent for building things, deep down in himself he wanted to own his own truck farm with a beautiful house, yard and garden. He wanted his wife to keep the flowers so pretty in the yard and on the porch just like his mother did. He did not ever want to have to do any farm work except his own. Gerald knew he could help build his own house and barn. He would raise hogs and cattle. He would not raise King Cotton. It seemed like too much work, too little certainty. Gerald made a good choice.

Jason, Sarah, and a New Suit

While Jason's mind was going over the children after he and Sarah prayed for all of them, Sarah's mind came back to him. She knew what she'd do tomorrow, for sure. She would write letters to the children, and Jason would surely get that suit in Kirksville. She said aloud to Jason, "Come on, my Jason. Let's go to bed and leave the Good Lord to do his work."

Jason was pleased when she talked like that. He hurried as he undressed to get in bed. He said, "You know, my Sarah, this bed has been so good to us. It is the same bed we slept in on our wedding night in 1898."

Sarah said, "Oh, my God! My God! It is the same bed fo' sure."

Jason said, "Remember though, we changed the mattress for several occasions."

Sarah laughed and said, "What mattress could last through 14 babies and many years?" Both laughed as they crawled into their double bed.

The Solleys had rested well. They were now ready for the new day. Jason made the kitchen stove fire. Sarah made the bed. As Jason started to the barn to take care of things there, Sarah said, "Jason, my Jason, tell me what you want for breakfast that I can fix fast."

Jason thought about yesterday's special breakfast of sage and red pepper sausage, pear preserves, fluffy biscuits and hot coffee. He called right back to her, "Can we have a repeat of yesterday's breakfast?"

Sarah was happy to say loudly, "We sho' can! Just give me about 40 minutes and get your hands washed. Can you make it?!"

"I will make it. Don't you worry none."

After breakfast was enjoyed, dishes washed, kitchen swept, churning of the milk done, Sarah said aloud to herself, "Now, Sarah Solley, get busy with those letters to the Solley bunch. You got to go meet the mail carrier today." With all that done and said, Sarah sat down to her tiny writing table in one corner of the big room to write. She put her ink bottle and fountain pen to her right and her writing paper and envelopes just in front of her. She thought again what she should say. They will each get the very same message. She would quickly remind them of their pa's faithfulness to the family, the church, the school, the Masonic Lodge and the colored people of Plum Creek Valley. She would remind them to remember that their pa (Daddy to those who had changed what they called him) had taught them to love God, love family, love reading, love respecting the law, love the privilege of going to vote, and love working toward a respectable life. She'd tell them that their pa needed to stop wearing mismatched suits when he dressed up. She would tell them how much the suit cost and how much each should send her by the end of the next week. She didn't want anybody slowing around either. They all knew their mother did not play.

Sarah finished her letters, but she knew she was out of stamps. She would meet the mail carrier at the mailbox up the road a piece, and give him the letters and her money for the stamps. He would take both, and he would do as was the custom out here. Many times people had to do this when they ran out of stamps. Sarah quickly changed into a different dress, grabbed her straw sun hat, checked the Grandfather clock, and walked swiftly to the mailbox. Yes, she could get there to meet him if she kept moving, she was thinking to herself. Jason always joked with her that she could move as fast as any of their children. She thought to herself, "I guess I can at that."

As Sarah walked back down the road home, she thought how she and the children were always so pleased when Jason would return from his once-a-year trip to the Grand Lodge. He unpacked his grip with the soiled starched shirts, soiled underwear, but no full suit. Yet he always managed to save enough of his spending money to bring just one present back home. Everybody knew who would get that one precious present. It would be their pa's special Sarah. He never forgot her. He never said, "Well, I wish I could have bought you a present, but my money ran out." If he had to do without anything, he never acted like it. He always was so happy to be back home.

Now Jason, thanks to their wonderful children, will own a nice new pin-stripe suit. Sarah knew all of the children well enough to be very sure that the ones who got those letters would send the money. She walked slowly home. She said to the Good Lord, "I thank you for helping Jason and me to raise good children. We have tried to do our best." She felt very good. She would not tell Jason just yet. She'd wait until the time was just right. It would be just right when she got all of the money next week. Then Jason was going to be made real happy. He was used to looking as good as we could make him at the time. Now, it has got to be another time. Yes, it was now time for another time! The time is for upgrading!

When Sarah went into her front gate, she was looking at the yellow rose bush on the left side of the walk to the steps. She turned her gaze to the red rose bush on the right side. Sarah called to Jason who was shucking corn in the first crib of a line of cribs. "Jason, come!" Sarah knew he would not just answer, but he would stop and come to see what it was.

Jason knew that she was especially happy. He said, "Sarah, my Sarah, what do you have?"

She was happy about two things. She said, "Have you noticed our rose bushes lately?"

Jason said, "Yes, I could see for a while that a full crop of roses were on their way. They are really pretty now. I'm glad you called me." Jason knew that Sarah was happy about something else, too. He would just wait until she talked.

After Jason went back to work in the barn, Sarah thought, "I almost told Jason that his grown children are just about to get him a brand new black pin-stripe suit. That would have been too much like a happy child. I almost spoiled the surprise. I didn't do it though." She walked out to the smokehouse, cut a small piece of cured hog meat from a shoulder that was half gone, and went back into the kitchen. She checked the coals in the cooking stove, added three sticks to the fire and put the meat in a small pot to boil. Sarah strung some green beans, washed them for the pot, and scraped a few Irish potatoes to add. She took a basket to the orchard, gathered fresh Alberta peaches to eat with their meal, and made a small plum cobbler. It was not time to eat yet, but everything would stay warm on the back of the stove.

Today would be a good day to just take off and go a'fishing. Jason could sho' use this time fishing. He would love to stop his barn work and just go. The crops were "laid by" for a few weeks. Sarah went to the nails on the back porch, took her sun hat off her nail, placed it squarely on her head and went to the barn. She called out from the gate as she unlatched it, "Jason, oh, Jason, come and eat! It's all ready for you. Then let's dig some red worms behind the barn, get in the wagon and go a' fishing."

Jason said, "Well, it sounds like a real good idea to me. I do get tired of doing what I need to do sometimes. It's a good time to do just what I want to do."

Sarah said, "I go wash my hands and serve our plates. Hurry now."

Jason said, "Coming right there, my Sarah."

After they had eaten Jason dug the worms for the bait, and Sarah washed the dishes.

Jason said, "I'll hitch up the wagon and bring it around. Meet me by the gate in ten minutes."

Sarah said, "I'll be right there. Be sure to bring my pole now."

Jason knew that everybody had their specific pole and hook to go fishing. He remembered that Sarah's had a red padding glued to the handle. It was very easy to spot. In just about ten minutes he pulled up to the front gate. Sarah was just a little late. She dashed down the steps with a small covered basket which contained a few fresh peaches in one hand, and a jar of water and cup in the other hand. She handed them up to him. Then she climbed up and into her seat. She felt excited. She felt free. She almost felt 19 again as she was the day she got married. Sarah never ceased to be happy when she had a special time with her Jason. Then it was extra good for her because the feeling was the same for Jason. Yes, she could feel it. She did not have to guess. Whenever they disagreed, and they sometimes did, they were both sure of one thing. It was that each would hear the other one out. Neither would try to out-talk or over-talk the other. When they could not reach an agreement, each knew that they had to seek an option. One would perhaps say, "I don't really see it that way, but since you feel so strongly that this is the way to go, then let us do." The other one then may just say, "Thank you." If the plan worked, then everybody was happy. If it didn't work, nobody was made to feel bad. Nobody would say, "See, I told you so." They respected each other.

The fish were biting in that particular portion of Plum Creek that day. Of course, Jason and Sarah had to move from two other spots to find this one. It was good that they had their mosquito smoking rags in the wagon. This fishing spot was dark because of so many trees and young bushes growing along the bank. The mosquitoes loved that better than the sunny spots. As the afternoon wore on, they accumulated enough fish to have a good mess for supper and breakfast in the morning. They did stop fishing and start home in time to scrape the scales, wash and salt the fish, milk the cows, put the livestock in their stalls, and fry the fish for supper. Fresh fish always made a good supper.

After all of the night work was shared, Jason and Sarah sat down to read and sew. They realized something had not been done yet. The lamp lights were too dim. Sarah discovered something fast. "Jason, our lamp globe cleaners and our coal oil fillers for our lamps are visiting their aunt Pearl. We have forgotten to do their jobs," Sarah said loudly.

"Well, that's so. We could not have gone much longer or we would be in almost total darkness," Jason said. Both of the Solleys laughed. Both got up out of their comfortable places. Jason said, "I'll fill the lamps with coal oil.." He started for the back porch to get the oil can. Sarah was on her way to get an old catalog from the back room to clean the lamp globes.

The sheets of the catalog could be crumpled to wipe inside the lamp globes after blowing her breath in the globe. This cleaning would last through week days. On Saturday the lamp globes were washed with vinegar water and dried with the same kind of crumpled paper until they sparkled. Sarah made their vinegar with apples.

Jason said, "Well, we will have to tell our last three children how much we missed them for many reasons." Then he laughed a hearty laugh.

Sarah joined him and said, "Well, it's been so many years since I had to clean the lamp globes, I had almost forgot how to do it." Of course, that was a real funny joke. She had done that in her own ma's and pa's house. She had done it in her house and Jason's before the children were big enough to do it. How in the world could she ever forget? She knew that she never could.

Once the house was all bright again, the Solleys settled down to finish what they had started. They read and sewed. Not much talking was going on now, but their kindred spirits were so much together. They did not have to talk for a while. As Sarah made her tiny stitches hemming dresses and patching knees and elbows on clothes, she wondered how any family survived without sewing and patching.

"Time goes fast and time goes slowly. It goes fast when you want it to keep on lasting. It goes slowly when you want it to hurry," Sarah said aloud one day after dinner.

Jason looked at her and smiled. Then he answered, "What in the world is my Sarah thinking about right now?"

She said, "Oh, just lots of things, lots of things. You and me have sure had good times together. Just you and me like when we first married. Yet, tomorrow we'll both be glad to see our last three born children. Their week will be up. We'll meet the train to get our Sophie, Claude and Edward. I know that their Aunt Pearl just spoiled them to death. Now they are coming back to the real world. I hope they know this, too." She laughed.

Jason added, "Well, if they don't know it when they get off that train, they'll sure know it before they go to sleep tomorrow night. You can bet on that." Sarah laughed loud. Jason laughed louder. They were happy.

Sarah was excited because the money had started to come in from the children for that suit. She could hardly contain herself. She just knew that the Solley children would all come through! The Pittsburg three boys had just outdone themselves. She could hardly keep it from Jason. Not only did they send their suit money, they sent their father a gold watch with the chain that fastens in the suit. Sarah was just bursting over. Every day she looked at the clock for mail time. She would almost run to the mail box.

Jason hitched up the wagon after breakfast, after the feeding and milking were done. They were going to meet the train. They were bringing their three youngest children home. As they rode along, they talked about how they were so thankful for their first 11 children to be doing well. They didn't know if they would have any children brave enough to want to be a farmer; yet Gerald had decided that he liked working the land and seeing things grow. He just wanted to be sure that the farm was his, and the house that his family lived in was his. He didn't want to farm if he had to sharecrop or live in a shack of a house. Gerald looked up to and held his own father as a good example of what he did want. He would brag to other people, "My daddy and my mother have surely taught me and my sisters and brothers about what not to settle for in this life in these United States of America." Gerald did much of his own home building. He had a right to feel good. His daddy Jason and his mother Sarah had taught them to love God, be honest, read and work hard. Gerald said to anybody interested enough to listen, "The Solley children are proud of their parents. We obeyed to love God, to be honest, to read, and we still don't mind working hard." Just because Gerald's words were true, there were railroad workers, school teachers, piano teacher, carpenters, Paris, France showgirl entertainer and a farm-owned farmer, Gerald himself. These made up the first 11 Solley children. The train station was very near now. It seemed like the children had been gone longer than a week.

Sarah and Jason had left the wagon at the hitching place and sat on the bench waiting. After a little while the train whistle let out a great shriek, and there it was coming to the station. Later Jason said to Sarah, "Do you think our children missed this train?" Both the parents hoped they hadn't got left..

Sarah said, "They got to be behind some of these people coming out, my Jason. Deep in her heart she had begun to wonder. They walked closer to the train, and then they screamed at the same time, "Oh, there they are! There are our children!"

Edward, the youngest, was the last getting off the train, but he was the very first to reach his parents. Next came Sophie. Claude brought up the rear. Everybody was running to meet each other. Oh, such a scrambling and hugging and kissing. Anyone looking on would think these people had not seen each other for a whole year. It was a great meeting. Each one of the young Solleys had carried their own small grip. Sarah had seen to that. Jason used his grip about once a year going to Grand Lodge meeting in some city, but nobody else used his grip.

They all got into the wagon and started the drive home. Sophie said, "Mother, Aunt Pearl sent you a present. Daddy, she sent you one, too. I know you both are going to like them."

Jason said, "Thanks, I can hardly wait."

Sarah looked back and said, "I know I'll have something to look forward to, but right now, I can see and enjoy my three runaways. My, my, it does seem like you have been gone longer than a week."

Claude and Edward were both taking in everything they passed on the road home. They were all happy.

"Edward," Sarah said.

"Yes, mother?" Edward answered.

"Tell me what you did that you really enjoyed the most. I mean the very, very most!"

Edward raised up in his seat and yelled really loud, "The carnival! We saw a man swallowing fire."

Sarah said, "What did Aunt Pearl think about a man swallowing fire?"

Edward said, "Well, she told us to not get too excited because that could be deathly dangerous if we tried that at home. She said that the man was just entertaining the people. She said not to ever, ever try that. She said things were not always the way they seem."

Sarah said, "I knew you had a very smart Aunt Pearl. That's why I felt satisfied for you to visit her." Then Sarah asked, "Claude, what did you enjoy the very, very most?"

Claude said, "Aunt Pearl took us to the Sanctified Church. The people danced and shouted. I had a good time watching."

Sarah said, "Why did you enjoy it so well?"

Claude answered, "I guess it was because I don't get to see that where we go to church."

To that, Sarah simply answered, "I see." Sarah asked Sophie the same question.

Sophie's answer was simple. She just said, "Mother, I enjoyed being with Aunt Pearl the most."

Sarah was pleased with all the answers. The children could all think for themselves. They did not have to give the same answer, but she learned something from each one of them.

Jason had just sat and drove the team of mules which pulled the wagon. He was thinking that he'd have plenty of time to find out lots of things within the next few weeks while the crops were laid by. There would not be much field work right now. Later schools would be back in session.

During the night the clouds that were gathering at bedtime poured down rain. They seemed to have emptied themselves of every drop of water they contained. Everybody was glad to be in bed in time to listen to the rain hit the window panes and the roof top. They slept well. Sometimes later the rain ceased. The clouds had been blown away and scattered by the soft summer wind. The morning broke through a clear sky, and the Solleys started crawling out of their beds. The only person in the house who had a room and a bed to herself at this time was Sophie. Claude and Edward, who had been born one year apart, shared a double bed in a room that might have once slept three or four Solley children. Now there were only three left this summer.

When schools opened in the fall, the household contents of Solleys would change again. Sophie would be entering Howard University in September. She was in her 18th year. Louise had attended Howard University. She was ten years older than Sophie, and was teaching high school English in Washington, D. C. Louise had made Howard University sound so enticing to Sophie. Of course, Sophie's high school English teacher had also attended there. Every day or two brought some new words of excitement from Sophie. She could hardly wait for September.

Jason said, "Sophie, do you understand fully why we are so excited for you and that college?"

Sophie answered, "Well, Louise graduated from that school, and it is an excellent Negro college."

Jason said, "Yes, that is right? But what other reasons can you think of?"

Sophie said, "My grades from high school earned me a good scholarship to Howard. I'll have to work part-time, but I don't mind that. If there is one thing all of the Solley children learned, it is how to work. It's been drilled into us to trust God and work for what we want. So I'd say you and Mother are proud of yourselves. It seems we have been learning our lessons pretty well."

Sarah had been busy, but now she wanted to get into this good conversation. She stopped churning the milk. She said, "Sophie, I think your daddy wants you to say that his own dream, a life-long dream, is being fulfilled by Louise and you. That's the school he dreamed of attending, but it didn't work for him." Sophie remembered her granddaddy had died suddenly.

Sophie said, "Daddy, I'm so sorry you didn't get to go to Howard, but I don't see how you would have done better in your life. You have always been such a good father. You take good care of our mother although she has worked hard too. She has the great satisfaction of knowing that you are always there for her." Jason smiled with happy understanding.

Sophie was making biscuits for breakfast. She had gone to the smokehouse and cut off exactly five pieces of side bacon. Everybody could tell which piece belonged to whom.

The largest piece was Jason's, the next was Sarah's the next Sophie's, then Claude, and then Edward. Since they didn't eat eggs every morning because Sarah peddled them in town, Sophie just fried the meat to eat with the biscuits, syrup, butter and milk. She also boiled coffee. Sarah looked at Sophie's pretty biscuits and said, "Sophie, you sho' can beat your mother with those biscuits." In her heart, she wanted reassurance. Sophie laughed. Then she hugged her mother and said, "Mother, I cannot beat you doing anything!"

Claude and Edward had been filling the washtubs and big pot with wash water. They had cleaned up the manure from the barnyard. They would now be ready for Sophie's breakfast. She called them in to wash up and eat. They ate like two hungry teenagers.

After breakfast the men folk went toward the barn and truck patches. The women finished the dishes and clothes washing.

Sarah's mind was on the mailbox. She expected the mail carrier to bring the last of the letters containing the children's money for Jason's suit. Just before mail time, Sarah recounted her suit money. She knew that today she could tell Jason that they could go back to Kirksville to purchase that suit. She had told the storekeeper her plan the day she went to the Madam C.J. Walker Hair place. She now would finish what she had started. Sarah arrived at the mailbox a few minutes early. She sat down on a pine stump. It was the stump that had seated many people waiting for the mail carrier. When she looked and saw his little Ford carrier coming up the dusty road, she sprang up from the stump. One other white woman had joined her at the mailboxes. The mail carrier placed the letters in the several boxes and tipped his cap. The he pulled off onto the dusty road. Sarah took her letters from the Solley box and slowly started sorting through as she walked up the lane. There were several letters, and yes, the ones she was expecting were in her hands. She stopped and sat on a knoll. She tore the ends off the letters, and besides the written words were the other important pieces. Yes, yes? There was so much more than enough for train fare, lunch and a suit. A new shirt, tie and shoes could also be purchased. Sarah could not walk to the Solley house. She ran all the way home. It was 1939, and Sarah was in her 60th year. Thank God, she felt good. She was still coming through the "change of life." Her hot flashes came and went just when they got ready to, but she felt that they were not so bad. She had often heard scary things about this time of life. But so far, she had not been scared yet. Some people thought that because her babies came for such a long time that it had shortened her "change of life" discomforts. Again, that was people talk. That was not doctor talk. At least, she did not hear of it from a doctor. She was glad.

Sarah's mind ran fast, but she ran faster. She had to find Jason. She had to tell him her good news. Jason was in the watermelon patch. She kept running until she found the patch. Sarah burst right out breathlessly, "Jason, oh my Jason, I have good news for you!"

Jason saw her excitement, and he started to meet her. He was becoming excited, too. He said, "My Sarah, my Sarah, what in the world is going on? Tell me now! Tell me right now!!"

Sarah said, "The Solley children have all let us know that they are Solleys. They have, all 11 who are grown, sent an answer of money for a brand new suit for you. Yes, that is just what they have all done! I asked."

Jason could only say, "When did all of this big thing happen? It is so special! How did you do it?"

Sarah looked up at Jason and smiled her famous smile. She said, "I just wrote them all a letter a piece. I told them about their wonderful daddy." She laughed and explained since they are not old-fashioned anymore, I said, "Your daddy, not your pa." Then Jason laughed. Sarah laughed again and again. No pa now, just daddy.

"Now Jason, don't plan to gather any watermelons or peaches tomorrow. Tell Claude and Edward what you want them to do in the barn or field. I'll tell Sophie what to do around the house. Of course, she has much sewing to do to get ready for school in a few weeks. She'll not need much prompting. That is one child who likes to look good," Sarah said.

Jason listened and said, "Sounds to me like Sophie is her mother's girl."

Sarah said, "Are you talking good or bad about me?"

Jason answered, "What could be bad about your daughter wanting to look good like her mother?"

Sarah said, "Well, if you put it like that, I guess I like it." She laughed.

"Now, can we get the train to Kirksville in the morning?"

Sarah could see Jason bursting open. "Yes, I can hardly wait. I must give you a whole lots of hugs and kisses for this good thing you did for me." Jason was really pleased about this.

The next morning everybody was up and moving early. The children had their instructions, and the grown-ups were going to have a very extraordinary day away. Again the train ride was enjoyable, and the Solleys could not get to the store fast enough after getting off the train. They walked a little faster this time than they had the other time. Their purpose was quite different. When they arrived at the store, Sarah did not hesitate, but bounded up the steps and right through the door. She explained her mission and was graciously waited on. Sarah had learned like many colored folks, and now Negroes, that when you had the money, the money had no color sense except green. Her money for the suit was very, very green! She looked around and beckoned Jason to come closer. The sales clerk looked him over and said, "Oh, yes, we can sure fit you up real good. If we were using real people to stand in the store window, you'd make a good one to show our clothes."

Jason and Sarah gave each other a knowing look. They both wondered if that was just the "green" in their money talking. Jason looked good though, but he was still a Negro. They purchased besides the suit, a shirt, tie and shoes. Yes, Jason was going to look so good next Sunday at the church, and when he went to the next Grand Lodge Masonic meeting in Little Rock. Sarah would be so proud of him. Now, he's the one getting a special present. All these years he had brought her back a special present.

They went by the hair dressing shop and made another appointment for Sarah's hair. This time they were very anxious to get home early. They stopped in at a hamburger shop and bought hamburgers and a grape and orange soda water. They were so good because both of them were hungry. They finished, caught the train and really did enjoy the ride home. The children were quite excited about their daddy's brand new clothes. They all wanted to see him in them. They were going to have to wait until Sunday. Jason did not want to do anymore trying on today. He was not used to this, but he was happy as he could be.

Sarah's Eastern Star Meeting

Sarah wanted to be at her Eastern Star Lodge meeting on time. She also wanted to have enough time to get her bath and take her time getting dressed. She hated bathing and dressing in a hurry. The women at the Lodge Meeting in Tall Point came from all over the area of Plum Creek Valley. Some of them took a little time with themselves and looked good. They made you feel good to see them come in the meeting Hall. Others looked so tacky until Sarah would almost feel sorry for them. She could not understand for the life of herself why some people did not seem to have no care for themselves. Sarah did not like to hear excuses that they didn't have time, or could not get into town to buy cloth to make a fresh dress, or they were afraid to go peddling in town, etc., etc.

"Jason, I don't understand for the life of me why some people so trifling. I'm glad you don't have to look at some people that I see. Now, there are others who make you feel real good. You don't need to feel sorry for them." Sarah said this because she wanted people to look happy. Jason knew that Sarah wanted always the best for everybody. That's why she is so loved. She does not want anybody to look like an underdog. He looked at her. He felt good that she was his wife and the mother of his children. He came close to her and said, "If you could, you'd bathe and dress everybody you thought needed it, wouldn't you?"

Sarah laughed, "No my Jason, I'm not that far into it. I do like to see people looking up though."

Sarah went to take her bath and dress. She would drive the buggy into town. A few people were driving cars like some of their children did, but she was going in her buggy. Jason would have it hitched up and ready by the time she got ready. What would she ever do without him? Everybody did not have a car in Plum Creek Valley in 1939. No, they simply did not. Sarah was doing all right. Her baby was 14. The next over him was 15. Her last girl was going to college real soon. How much more could she ask the Good Lord for. She thought that she would only ask for a good bath.

After Sarah got her tub with lots of warm water and real bath soap, she closed the doors to her area. Everyone knew that he or she must find another way to wherever was the destination because it was bath time. Sarah finished and stepped into a pretty one-piece blue and white broadcloth dress that she had taken the time to make it look exactly like the one she saw in the Sears and Roebuck Catalog. She wore her hair brushed up all the way around to the very center of the top. There she made a chignon by wrapping the hair around and around and pinning it securely. She put on her white Cuban heel pumps. She carried her white handbag which held pen, note pad, coin purse and peppermints. Her meeting would start at one o'clock. She was going to be in plenty of time. Already her buggy seat was covered with old clean quilts, and her umbrella stayed under the seat. The buggy top would be pulled if needed. Otherwise, she would just carry the umbrella when she got out if it was necessary. She hoped it wouldn't be.

Sarah was the secretary of this local group of Eastern Stars. She had learned how to listen and take notes many years before. When she was fourth and fifth grade, her teacher seemed to have thought she had a special talent for taking notes or keeping any kind of class records. She had held the position of Sunday School secretary in her Methodist Episcopal local church until she became too busy with the little Solleys. Sarah was early enough to get herself settled at the officers' table. Now she could watch other folk come in, and this she really did like. She told herself to be careful about looking too closely and perhaps being a little too critical. Sarah genuinely liked meeting with this group of women. They were, for the most part, people with good hearts and kindly dispositions. When the meeting was over, some would buy a few things after leaving the Hall. Others would do as Sarah would do, go straight home. They came from far and near in Plum Creek Valley.

When Sarah arrived home, Sophie had food cooking for supper. Fourteen-year-old Edward had gotten a chicken out of the coop in the back yard, wrung its neck and dressed it for Sophie. Claude had brought in fresh corn from the patch, shucked it and cut it off the cobs. Sophie cooked green beans, made a small plum cobbler and cornbread.

The smothered chicken was still simmering. The other food was slowly cooking, but almost ready. Everything smelled good. The aroma coming from the kitchen reminded Sarah that she had not eaten since breakfast. She was just about ready for all of this. Jason had heard her driving up and came to meet her at the barn gate. He had been shelling corn, but now it was quitting time for the night. He greeted his Sarah just the same way she greeted him. They acted like they had not seen each other for two or three days. Why did she love him so much? Sarah thought. Sarah said, "Hi there, my Jason!"

"Hi, my Sarah. I see you made it back safe and sound. You had a good meeting at the Hall?"

"It was better than ever. We all liked seeing each other again, and we made a lot of progress with where we left off last meeting. Yes, it was a very good meeting, I'd say." They warmly embraced.

"I'll put the mule and buggy away and be right in."

"Thank you for always taking good care, Jason." Sarah went on to the kitchen. She didn't bother going around the front. It was closer to the kitchen though the back door. Also, that's where those hungry-making smells were coming from. "I'm back, gang. How's everything been going?"

Sophie and the boys said almost together, "Hi there, Mother!" One by one they came to embrace Sarah.

Edward said, "We missed you. Did you have any time to miss us?"

"I always have time to miss my favorite people," Sarah said.

Sarah was looking forward to seeing her Jason in his brand new suit Sunday. Everybody was going to church the next day. Therefore, the night work was completed just a bit earlier because the Sunday School lessons needed to be studied entirely or reviewed. The baths were to be taken and maybe some clothes needed to be pressed. Everybody in this house knew that there never was an excuse to be late for Sunday School. Sarah made sure that Jason's things had all been made tag free. She did not want him sitting or standing with a price tag or label showing on any of his new clothes tomorrow. Claude and Edward knew how to press their clothes and polish their shoes. Sarah had taught her sons to take care of their daddy's shoes. Jason never had to be concerned with this little chore once the older boys got big enough. Now that only the two baby sons were left in the home, it seemed that Jason would have to return to his old job. These boys were soon going off to school.

Sarah teased her husband saying, "Oh, now, my Jason. What are you going to do? Your last two shoe-shine boys will soon be going away to high school?"

"Some things once learned and practiced are never forgotten. I guess polishing and shining shoes is just one of those things. I'm sure my feet won't have to be embarrassed because I forgot what I knew for so many years. Now, what do you say to that?" Jason said.

"Well, you have stumped me there. I have to agree that as good as you knew how to make your feet look, you could never forget how to do it."

After spending a very good morning at church on Sunday, the Solleys found their various ways of relaxing. Sarah caught up on her Bible reading and sharing the *Plum Creek Valley Chronicle* with Jason. Then she opened their little home library, took out the well-worn copy of Louisa M Alcott's *Little Women*. This book had been given to her by her teacher when she was fifth grade. She had read it, and all the girls had read it. Now she felt like reading it again. Jason was reading again the *Book of Job*. He said that he was always given renewed strength when he took time to study this Old Testament story.

Sophie's beau, Andrew Walker, came out from Tall Point to spend time with her. He drove his daddy's Chevy Truck, and was so pleased with himself because many young Black men still did not get this opportunity at that time. They sat on the porch in the swing and worked crossword puzzles. Claude and Edward went to the Pine Hill Grade School playground to play baseball with some other boys in the neighborhood.

Jason and Sarah were feeling like their family was indeed blessed. At one time they had a few very private misgivings about their "Dreamer" Hazel, entertainer and show girl. Now they were pleased that she had been discovered in a Tall Point Talent Show. Then went to work in New York, and from there to Paris, France's stage. Hazel was doing all right. At one point Sarah had asked her husband, "Do you think that our Hazel intends to be our stray chicken from the yard?" Jason had stopped whatever it was that he did. He came closer to his wife and the mother of his children. He reached out and caught both of her hands in his big overworked hands. Then he looked straight into her eyes and said, "My dear Sarah, we have done our best to teach our children about right and wrong. They have learned to trust us and our best judgment. We have taught them to trust their own judgment in this life. We have taught them more to trust God, and that's the most important of all the trusting. We now have to trust Hazel. She will be all right." Sarah thought for a brief moment. "My Jason, thank you for talking some sense into my head. What you just said makes more sense than my doubting. Hazel will be all right."

There was a black Ford speeding up the road. At the corner it slowed down considerably and turned in toward the Solley house. Well, it was Gerald, the Solleys' farmer boy. He had been the only one of the Solleys who picked farming as his life's work. He and his wife and two girls were enjoying their home and cattle and truck patch farm. Gerald did not change his mind about not growing cotton, but the other things kept thriving and thriving. He had a talent for this.

Gerald offered to take his mother and father for a ride into town, but the older Solley declined because this Sunday afternoon had already been planned just the way it had been going. They promised their younger children that they would be home this afternoon. Sarah brought her visiting son and family peach cobbler and buttermilk for a repast. She also brought out Jason's brand new clothes. She knew that Nancy would enjoy this even more than Gerald. She loved to see people look good. She praised her husband's parents to everybody she knew. She felt that they were special people in so many ways. She and her Gerald had been some of the very first Solleys to reply to Sarah's request for the new full suit outfit. She was the kind of girl that the older Solleys considered another daughter. Gerald had always had a tendency to want to have his own way, but Sarah had noticed with silent approval that Nancy could hold him in check. He wasn't stubborn with her, it seemed. She was what he needed. He respected her opinion because of her very strong will.

Sophie

President Franklin D. Roosevelt had been elected into office in 1932, and by 1939 many Negroes were feeling that they had benefited by his presidency. Young folk felt the positives as well as older folk. The NYA was especially beneficial to Negro students, many of whom had to go off to high school and needed all the help they could possibly get. After-school jobs were welcomed. Many a girl, especially Negro girls, pushed the big brooms to clean class rooms after school, and some did anything else available to get the NYA check which helped them to be able to stay in school.

Sarah would say to Jason, "I don't know how this family would make it without Mr. Roosevelt's rules and regulations. Do you, my Jason?"

Jason would readily agree and say, "In my honest opinion, President Franklin D. Roosevelt is one of our lifesavers."

Sarah continued, "There will some day be more laws for making high schools and colleges easier for Negro children to attend, especially the ones who live out in the country."

Jason answered, "Yes, I foresee transportation getting better and the school districts starting to do more to accommodate all of the students. I hope our President stays in office a long time."

Jason and Sarah were visualizing a bright future for all of

their grandchildren, great-grandchildren and on and on down the line. They could see all Negro children getting farther and farther away from the negative effects of the long, long arms of slavery. Jason was now in his 64th year. He had experienced many ups and downs in these years, but he was quick to say there had been more ups than downs.

Sarah would often say to Jason, "The Good Lord sure did answer my prayer and made you my husband." Being always moved by his wife's open show of admiration and affection, Jason would reach out for her and pull her close to him. She could still cuddle.

Sophie had been spending time getting her wardrobe ready for school. She had also been doing lots of reading and part-time work for two white ladies in the area of Plum Creek Valley. She went to their homes and did cleaning, cooking and dishes. They knew that Sophie was Jason and Sarah Solley's daughter. Because they thought so highly of them, they paid Sophie well. They agreed to do whatever they could to help the Solley girl be able to go off to Howard University in Washington, D.C. She would never be any threat to them. She had told them that she wanted to become a lawyer and that, of course, meant extra years of school. These women agreed with each other, "We will help the Solley girl. She is nice and she is smart." Sophie needed more luggage and more substantial luggage to go away. She wanted to pick pieces that would hold up for all the years she would be in school. Sarah suggested, "Sophie, why not get a nice trunk that will hold almost all of your things? I think that is better than buying suitcases. Just have a nice small suitcase for your personal small things."

Sophie listened to her mother. Her mother made good sense. But didn't she always make good sense? "Mother, that's the best idea! I can check the trunk on the train, and I can keep the little suitcase."

"Everything you'll need until your trunk is back with you will stay with you," Sarah said.

Sophie and Sarah were telling their plans to Jennie Baker, who was always ready to hear good news and to offer a helpful suggestion. Jennie listened carefully, and then she called out loudly, "I just thought of something, Sarah! Oh, listen to this! The white lady that I go weekly to clean for has two good-looking trunks in her attic. They look almost like new. I bet she'd be just so glad to give Sophie one of them."

Sarah got excited. She said, "Jennie, do you think she'd be willing to give it instead of selling it?"

Jennie Baker said, "This woman likes to see young Negroes who are worth something do good with their lives."

Sarah answered, "Thank you, thank you. Would you ask her about this?"

Sarah was really excited because Sophie needed to save all the money that she could. If she didn't have to buy a trunk, that would sho' be a real help.

Jennie said to Sarah, "I will be going to my lady's house in the morning. When I leave there before noon, I'll sho' 'nuf have the answer. I believe in my heart it'll be the right answer, too. I let you know tomorrow."

Sophie had not had a chance to get a word in until now. She said, "Mrs. Baker, you will be a lifesaver if you can get me that trunk. Well, I don't mean it will exactly save my life, but it will certainly help me to get ready for school. Thank you so much for even thinking of this, and for offering to help."

Jennie Baker just said, "You such a nice girl."

Sophie then added, "Now, I can see where my very great brother-in-law, Joe, gets so much of his sweetness."

Jennie chuckled and said, "That sho' is a good thing to say, Sophie."

Sophie said further, "Well, when it's time for me to find a husband, I do hope he'll be something like my sister Nona's husband, Joe."

Jennie Baker said, "Oh, I bet you will find him, now. Joe is a good boy."

"I sure hope I do." Sophie answered.

The next afternoon Jennie Baker and her husband Frank came driving up with the trunk. Sarah and Sophie hugged and hugged Jennie. Jason came out and helped Frank unload the beautiful like-new trunk. It was more than the Solleys expected.

Claude and Edward

Attendance to a one-room, one-teacher school sometimes meant that children a year or two apart in age ended up in the same classes. Therefore, they would be finishing the eighth grade at the same time. It often happened that way. This was true with Claude and Edward Solley. Both would be entering Sampson High School in Tolletville, Arkansas, in September of 1939. Edward was the youngest, yet he was more scholarly. He looked for new books to read all of the time. He did his homework without any prompting from Jason. He needed no promises from Sarah.

With Claude, it was a harder job. He would do his school work only when he had done everything else that he could possibly think of to do first. Somehow he always had his work done when it was time for him to turn it in or make an oral report. For this habit of procrastinating, Jason was not really pleased. Sarah wrote down her ideas of how they might handle this. Then she promptly tore the paper into very small pieces because she got another idea. She hurried to find Jason and she blurted out, "I just thought of something about Claude and the way he seems to hate to study his school work." Sarah felt a new inspiration.

"What did you think of, my Sarah?" She looked up toward the sky and then came out with "The Good Lord gave

Claude a good mind, right?"

"Yes, I'd say that is right."

"He does use it all right most of the time, doesn't he?"

"I'd say that is right, too. Now what are you coming to?

"I think we need to start thanking the Good Lord a whole lot more and start expecting just a little less from our children because God has maybe spoiled us just a little bit. We expect a whole lot from all of our children. They do well at most everything they set out to do. Yes, you and me have pulled all of them a whole lot. I think we may just ought to let them see how much we trust them to do what we have taught them to do. We can afford to ease up a little."

Jason looked at his Sarah with new eyes and also with a brand new sense of respect. He knew that his wife had a very sharp mind. He knew that she was sensitive, kind and loving. Now she was expressing a side that pulled up her deep, deep spirituality. His heart was pounding in his chest. He went close enough to his wife to pull her into his arms, and he said, "My Sarah, my Sarah. I cannot do or say anything more to improve your thoughts and your deep convictions. I must agree with what you have just said. Also, I could not have said it as well. Beginning right now. I am going to start thinking some new thoughts. I am going to stop letting myself believe that our children will not be all right if we let up a little. All of the others have shown us that they could choose their own routes. This should be enough to satisfy us. We cannot measure and compare Claude and Edward because it is not fair. Thank you for making me see clearly. I do say thank you a whole lot."

Canning and Syrup Making

It was peach canning day. Sarah knew that today every Solley who was left at home would be contributing to filling jars and more jars of peaches. Jason and the boys went into the orchard and filled bushel baskets with tree-ripened succulent peaches. Sophie drew water to wash and cook them with. Sarah washed and sterilized the glass fruit jars. At one time, she was the only one to fill and seal the fruit jars, because a certain amount of care needed to be taken to assure perfect canning. Otherwise, a lot of jars of peaches might be lost through spoilage. She soon started teaching this.

Now it was time for everybody to sit on the back porch with sharp knives and peel and cut up carefully washed peaches. After they were cooked in a small amount of water for a required length of time, the prepared jars were quickly filled and sealed. Some days 30 or 40 jars were completed and placed on the canning shelves in the back room. These peaches would be eaten for breakfast fruit and for dinner and supper cobblers all through the winter. Since the family had gradually dwindled, Sarah did not need to can as much of anything as she used to do. However, she didn't forget to send buckets of peaches to needy people in the Plum Creek Valley neighborhood. She also peddled some in town. Peddling was still a sure way to earn a few quarters. Quarters added up to dollars pretty good and pretty fast, too.

The Great Depression of the late '20s and early '30s made a whole lot of people, and especially Negroes, learn how to take advantage of every opportunity to help make ends meet. The Solleys had a family which had always required them to count pennies and stretch quarters.

With the canning day behind them for a while, it was time for attention to be put to the cane which had been growing beautifully for the syrup to be made. It had been planted, tended, and now was cut down by Edward, Claude and Jason. Then they hauled it in the wagon to Jason's mill just on the other side of the pond outside the barnyard. It was a very interesting process to be a part of and watch. Jason made the wood fire under the sorghum pan. The boys hitched the mule to the mill and started feeding the long stalks of cane into the mule-powered mill. The mule walked around and around the mill as the juice was being caught in a huge container. The second boy kept taking the cane juice to Jason at the mill. Jason kept a close watch and careful pushing of the cane juice until the juice had been gradually moved from one end of the cooking divided pan to the other. The result was beautiful honey-colored syrup by the gallons and gallons. Jason really knew how.

Jason made syrup for lots of farmers in Plum Creek Valley. He sold many gallons every year. Selling syrup helped the family with school expenses well as supplying the table. White folk liked and bought Jason Solley's good syrup.

The Great Depression

The Great Depression and stock market crash of 1929 had exhibited such far-reaching implications. Even though Black people didn't have as much to lose as so many white people, their losses were still very devastating to them. The long arm of the great losses reached through whites to give a resulting hard blow to so many Negroes, many of whom had mortgaged their modest homes for much needed ready cash flow. When they were not able to pay as they had promised, there were foreclosures. Many Negroes moved and cried bitter tears. Some in the area of Plum Creek Valley had to move into old rundown empty shacks. Some crowded into the homes of relatives and friends. This was supposed to be only temporary measures, but sometimes they became much too permanent for too long. Some Negroes who never would have even dreamed of it had to sharecrop on a white owner's farm because they could see no alternative.

Jason and Sarah managed to remain on their farm and keep their livestock. The Solley children always found work in some white person's house, yard, garden or field. They always stayed plenty busy. Their parents thanked God that they knew how to work and that they didn't mind working. They always believed that the steps they were making at a given time were simply stepping stones to where they really wanted to go. As long as the children believed in this concept, their feet would remain planted on solid ground. Always at the Solley house, prayers had sustained them (the home prayers before meals, morning, and night and also the Sunday worship prayers).

Jason, Claude, and Edward

One day Jason took Claude and Edward into town to buy a few needed clothes for school. As they rode along the graveled road, they enjoyed seeing early signs of fall. In the wagon bed were some late summer sweet corn, fresh green black-eyed peas, late watermelons, turnip greens by the bundles, and fresh tomatoes. These items would go fast when they peddled them in town. Of course, there were always the regular customers. If anything was left, it went very fast as well. All three in the wagon enjoyed the outdoor scenery of a few leaves turning red and gold. The birds were flittering from tree to tree. Squirrels ran up the trees as though they were being chased. Some stray-looking cat would cross the road in a hurry, just barely missing being stepped on by a mule's foot. Now and then a rabbit's white cotton tail could be glimpsed going between some bushes. These things were just a small part of the enjoyment of a wagon ride into Tall Point on a lazy afternoon. They soon sold all of their fresh farm-raised wares. Now they checked their list of needed items and began looking for the best bargains in town. They completed a satisfactory job.

As Jason and the boys were on their way to the wagon, they approached a group of people near their wagon talking very excitedly. One walked toward Jason and said, "Jason, we have just heard some bad news. John Sullivan just returned home from a business trip to Little Rock and found his wife murdered." Jason could not believe his own ears.

"Murdered!" Jason replied.

"Shot right through the head, the police said. She was found in their bedroom and had been dead for a few hours," the man continued.

"Who would want to do a thing like that to Miss Amy? I cannot imagine her having enemies that mean. She was such a kind and generous-hearted lady. My girls always benefited from her goodness. She had the prettiest clothes which she would hand out to Louise, Mindy and Hazel as they went off to school. She didn't make them work for them. She always said she liked them for trying to be somebody. We are so sorry to hear this bad thing. Do they have any suspects, any clues at all?" Jason asked.

"If they do, they're not telling yet. You bet they are going to be real busy. Plum Creek Valley not used to having too much bad trouble," the man said.

"I know my family will be very upset. Thank you for telling us." Jason was really very disturbed.

As Jason and the boys were driving home, the boys who had remained quiet now started to talk. Both had evidently been listening carefully. Edward was the first to speak saying, "Wonder why the killer wanted to wait 'til Mr. Sullivan was so far away to kill his wife? I wonder did he have something against Mr. Sullivan or something against Miss Amy?"

Edward was looking from his daddy to his brother. He was listening hard for a word from either one because that question was burning inside his head.

Jason spoke, "I'm going to let your brother go first. You boys are younger and could have fresher ideas than I have. I must say, Edward, that you have asked a very important question though. I bet the police are asking that very same question to each other." They both now looked at Claude, who was one year older than Edward.

Claude laughed and said, "Well, I was hoping you two would do this police work and let me just listen to the two detectives at work."

Edward answered, "We not letting you off so easy. Come on with your answer. You must have one."

Claude said, " I was thinking suppose the killer didn't wait until Mr. Sullivan was far away."

"What do you mean, Claude?" Edward asked excitedly.

"I mean just what I said, Maybe the killer was not far away because maybe the killer was Mr. Sullivan himself," Claude spoke assuredly.

Now Jason could not hold his voice any longer. He said, "Claude, do you really think that could be? Why would he want to murder his nice wife?"

Claude could readily see that he had struck a heavy chord where his daddy was concerned. He took his time and calmly answered his daddy. He looked from his daddy to his brother and answered, "Well, it was you, Daddy, who said that thing about his nice wife. Maybe Mr. Sullivan did not think she was such a nice wife. Maybe he didn't really go to Little Rock. Maybe he just pretended to be gone that far. Maybe he hid somewhere until the right time."

Jason's mouth was standing wide open. He was thinking fast now. He had another question for this 15-year-old son who was just starting high school. He looked at Claude and said, "Can you think of what might have been deemed a right time for this man to kill his wife?"

Claude said, "I read a story that made me think of this

man who thought his wife had a beau on the side, but he couldn't prove it. He kept trying to catch his wife. I thought this might be what Mr. Sullivan was trying to do by pretending to go away. According to my sisters, Miss Amy was real pretty and bought lots of pretty clothes. When she had worn them a while, she bought more new clothes and gave old ones to them. Miss Amy didn't have to work the same as lots of other women." Claude stopped right there to catch his breath.

Edward cut in and said, "My goodness, Claude, you do have a great big imagination. Don't you think so, Daddy?"

Jason was not only totally captivated, but he was spellbound. His 15-year-old solving or possibly solving a crime. He said to Claude, "I must say that you do have some thoughts here that could be very, very serious. However, let me advise you to not share your theory with any of your friends. Can either of you boys tell me why I say this?" The two boys turned and looked at each other.

Edward said, "Is it because Claude could get in trouble with some white people for this kind of talk? It would be dangerous. Even though he could be right, he better not ever be saying it away from our house. Somebody might find him shot through the head just like Miss Amy. Right, Daddy?"

Jason had really listened. He answered Edward, "I think you have a good answer. I don't see how I can improve on it, and ,Claude, you might think of studying law and become a detective when you grow up."

Claude said, "Are you serious, Daddy? I hope you are because I do like to try to figure things out. Who knows, I might one day be a super detective. I could be a good lawyer."

Edward said, "Yes, and one day I just might be President of these United States of America, too."

Claude said, "Don't make fun of me. I am dead serious. Plum Creek Valley will smile on me."

Edward answered, "So it will. We are getting farther and farther away from slavery every day. We are getting better educated and will have a better place. You ought to seriously consider being in the law business, Claude."

Claude was thinking that maybe he would study law. Of course, the more you stayed in school the more money you needed. Well, then he'd just have to excel in his school work and become eligible for good scholarships. Also, he could always get a job to help himself. Yes, the Solley family didn't mind working to get what they really wanted. He wanted to study law.

Claude stopped thinking and said with determination, "This is not a joking matter. I believe I will study law."

Jason sat up a little taller in the wagon seat. He said, "Claude, it's not too early for you to get some ideas about what you want to do. You do have time to change your mind if you find something else more to your liking."

Edward cut in and said, "Yes, Claude, you'll be the kind of lawyer that might fool the right people and then you'll win the case."

"What do you mean by that?" Claude asked.

"You'll be acting like you are not working hard at all on the case. Then you come up and win the case because you were working hard just like you do now. You come up at the last minute with all your homework done or your reports all ready."

Jason was remembering that fact. He spoke up and said, "Well, I'll declare. I didn't know that you had noticed that, too." They all laughed.

Joe Jr., Sophie, Claude, Edward

Joe Baker, Jr. and his young Aunt Sophie had a quite unusual situation since they were only a few months apart in age. Joe's grandmother Sarah was pregnant at the same time that her daughter Nona was, but Joe was born first. Now they were going off to college at the same time, but to different colleges. Sometimes they acted more like sister and brother. Joe, Jr. was going to AM&N College in Pine Bluff. He was going to major in mathematics. He seemed to have inherited his grandfather Jason's ability for and love of math. Now, he was visiting with Jason.

Jason said to him, "What do you plan to do with all your mathematical learning?" He listened carefully for the answer.

Joe, Jr. said, "Right now I see myself teaching high school algebra and geometry. Since I love it so much and I made very high grades, I felt this perhaps should be the way to go. There is still time for me to make a final decision, wouldn't you say, Granddaddy?"

Jason said, "That sounds good enough to me for now. Once you get to school and really get into everything, there might be other things that look more appealing to you. You can never tell."

Joe, Jr. said, "Well, Granddaddy, I always know I can depend on you for an honest, thoughtful opinion. As I go along,

I'll be checking in with you from time to time because I feel good when I talk with you."

Jason was, of course, pleased to talk with his grandson.

He looked at Joe, Jr. and could see a whole lot of his grandmother Sarah. If he could keep her quiet sensible way of thinking, that was really in his favor. Jason also could see Joe, Jr.'s grandmother Jennie's kind ways. He could see his granddaddy Frank's gentle ways. This young man could go far as long as he did not forget his God and his roots. Jason felt happy.

His girl Nona had not done bad for herself to see the good in this boy's daddy when he was under the critical eyes of many in this Pine Hill Grade School area of Plum Creek Valley. There had been a time when Sarah and Nona had eyes that allowed them to see farther than most about the potentials of the Bakers. Even though Nona was quite young at the time, she was still very perceptive. She later would laugh and claim that she could see way back there that Joe Baker was going to be her very own husband. She didn't hear what anybody else might have said. She just knew that this boy with the rough-looking edges was only just that (rough-looking, not really and truly rough). Nona, like her mother Sarah, was exactly right.

Now Joe Jr. and Sophie would be boarding the trains soon to enter their first year of college. Sophie had done a good job of working to earn extra money, sewing, and slowly packing her very own spacious trunk. She had been careful to work well in whatever she did. She had been told that various jobs would be available to her whenever she needed to work again while attending college. However, Nona was looking forward to continuing part-time work during the summer in Washington, D. C. It was good to know that she could also come home and work if it became necessary. The Solley children were taught to work at any job with respect for the job and the one that they worked for.

Sarah always said to the children, "Even if you don't like the job or if you don't like the one you are working for, respect yourself and do the kind of job that is a credit to you! Do the kind of job that will make you feel good about yourself! Do the kind of job that will make God pleased with you!"

Sophie was glad that she had heard her mother. She did feel good about whatever she did for anybody because it was right to do it right. Sometimes that had been the only reason she did it.

Claude and Edward would not be going to the one-room Pine Hill Grade School. They had been looking forward to going "off to school." The time had almost arrived. They would be getting on the bus and staying in Tolletville, Arkansas, to attend the high school there. They would come home for special holidays.

Jason wanted them to understand something. So he said seriously, "Now, boys, you are growing up, and you have to start acting like you are. Why am I saying this?" Jason looked from Claude to Edward.

Edward spoke, "I think it's because we are soon going to be living apart from our two parents who keep us straight. So we have to grow up."

"Claude, the turn is now yours. Can you add or subtract anything from that?" Jason continued.

I think when you said that we have to start 'acting like' we are growing up, that's not so scary as it sounds at first. 'Acting like' just means we have to speak sensibly and not be silly and foolish acting. It doesn't mean that we got to grow suddenly into old men, does it, Daddy?" Claude asked with great concern.

Jason appreciated the extra bit of thought and the sincere desire for more clarification on this. He looked at Claude and he looked at Edward. Then he said, "Edward, I liked your answer. Claude, I liked your answer, too, because both of you are right. 'Acting like' doesn't mean you have to stop being your age. It won't take away any of the clean fun that you would normally have, but you must always know how far to go without having your own parents to guide you. It means that you will always be willing to listen to and obey those who are in charge of you at the boarding home. It will mean that your mother and I will not ever expect to get anything except good reports about you. Of course, you are letting us see all the time that we shouldn't have to worry about you." Jason knew exactly how to get the best out of his children. He showed his concern for them. He also expressed his confidence in them.

Claude said, "Well, since I am one year older than Edward, does he have to obey me?" Claude laughed and laughed hard. He knew he'd get a response from Edward. Yet Edward said not a word. He was looking at his daddy.

Jason said, "This new situation will not make you Edward's daddy or mother. Understand?"

"Yes, Daddy. I do understand."

Fall 1939

Jason and Sarah had seen the bus go off with their last two boys and had seen the train go off with their last girl. They had seen another train go off with their first grandson. Right now, they felt like their house was as near empty as it had been on their wedding day. They had gone to the bus and train stations with a whole lot of great joy and thanksgiving.

One day Sarah said, "We may seem like we are back where we started, Jason, but we can never really go back there again, can we?"

Jason laughed and then joked, "Well, it was just us two when we came in here the day we got married, and it's just us two right now, ain't it?"

"Yes, that part is right. Not even our love for each is the same anymore," Sarah added.

"Why in the world do you think that, my Sarah?"

"Because our love for each other has grown bigger and bigger and bigger. It covers our 14 children, too," Sarah said.

Jason thought for a moment and then he added, "You know, my Sarah, at one time in my young life I thought I had been cheated because my pa died and my plans necessarily and drastically changed. Now when I think of that and think of what the change did for my life, I do feel truly grateful that God has taken charge of my life all along. Things came out just the way they were meant to. Howard University would or could have made me a better educated man, but who's to say that my purpose in life would have been served? When I look at you, my Sarah, I have to believe that I couldn't have led a more useful and satisfactory life." He looked toward Sarah with love. Sarah reached for his hand and moved close to him. They were quiet now.

The orchard's late peaches were dark red. They were beckoning for some attention as they had started to drop one by one to the ground. Here was a job that both Sarah and Jason would start putting their attention to. These beautiful peaches, called Indian peaches, were welcomed for just eating the succulent but firm flesh, and for canning because there never was too many canned peaches. In town they always made fast-selling peddling wares. Most of the locally grown fresh peaches had long been gone. Sarah went to get her straw sun hat as Jason went to get some bushel baskets. In one accord they went to the orchard just outside the yard. They acted like two children as they couldn't resist the urge to pick up tree-ripened peaches and eat and eat. Finally, Jason stopped eating to say, "You can sure tell that these are getting close to the last peaches of the season. We are eating them as though we haven't had a peach this year."

Sarah stopped, swallowed, and then she said, "I think our stomachs must be feeling that soon this kind of feast will all be over until next year."

Jason said, "What a dreary thought! But on the other hand, it's a delicious thought!" At that they both laughed. Then they started filling the baskets. They picked up the ones on the ground first and put all of them in a small basket. Then they started to pull the ripened peaches from the trees. When they had finished pulling all that were sufficiently ripened, they took them to the back porch to "cull" them out. That process was to ensure they carried nothing but the best ones to town to sell. The ones that needed further work remained home for Sarah to start making preparations to can for the winter. She was always thankful that years ago Jason had had enough good sense to provide for the family that he did not yet have. Oh, yes, she thought, her Jason had always been a thinking man.

As Sarah started getting the peaches ready for Jason to take to town, he drew up water to wash Sarah's peaches to start canning preparation. Oh, yes, this was a full time job for everybody, and they understood that working fast together was how to get the job done. Jason helped peel and cut up peaches for a time. Then when they had prepared enough to get started, Jason made the fire in the kitchen stove for sterilizing the fruit jars. After he had helped Sarah get started, he went and hitched up the wagon. Promising to get back as soon as he could, Jason rode to town. He had no delays with his peddling. Soon his baskets were empty and his wallet was feeling pretty good. He sprang up into the wagon, caught the reins and said, "Git up, git up" and quickly rolled away. As he hurried home, Jason thought that he'd be doing this or Sarah would be bringing eggs and fresh butter every time the opportunity presented itself. That's how they had managed over the years. They saw no reason to stop this now with children out of the home, but still in school. As the team of mules brought the wagon into the barn, Jason stepped briskly to the ground and felt whole.

Sarah had cooked and sealed many jars of peaches. She had also peeled and cut up more while the first batch was cooking. She was glad to see Jason for three reasons. He had sold out in town, he could help her finish all of these peaches, and she still loved him enough to be glad to see him each time he returned home. Jason and Sarah greeted each other warmly, put the day's till in their joint private "bank" under the head of their bed.

Jason said to Sarah, "You did a lot with the canning while I was gone. There is not so much left to do."

She answered, "You had helped get it all started. I just kept it moving best I could. We'll have time to get the feeding and milking done outside, the cooking and churning inside. Then we can eat a little early and read a while before bedtime."

Jason was pleased with the sound of that. Both of them did look forward to relaxing after the evening meal.

The Solleys looked forward to their mailman's coming each day. This looking for the mail became more and more intense as more and more Solleys left home. They had helped the children know how important it was to stay in touch. In a little while it would be 1940. They still did not have Mr. Alexander Graham Bell's miraculous invention. The telephone kept evading them because something else just kept on coming before it. This is what Sarah always said, "The poor Negroes in Plum Creek Valley keep on finding something else to do with that telephone money, but one of these days maybe enough of us will see fit to put some of our money into a telephone. Right now, we are busy trying hard as we can to get our children educated, and that will put them in a better condition to do more things the way a lot of white people do right now."

Jason would never ignore Sarah's claim because he was in total agreement with her. He'd usually answer this way, "You know, my Sarah, I couldn't have said that half as well as you did. Anybody can see plainly that you really believe we should know what should come first as we live. Then we should do the most important things first."

When the Solleys were reading after the evening meal, it suddenly came to Jason that they had gotten too busy to remember the mailbox today. Once in a while they had days like that. As he turned another page and was really enjoying his reading so much, he decided not to even mention this to his Sarah. He did not want her wanting him to go to the box now. He sure was not going to allow her to go. He just smiled to himself and kept on quietly reading. He felt sure they would be none the worst for missing the mail. If there was something urgent, the writer would call the nearest white neighbor who would be kind enough to deliver the message to Jason and Sarah. With that thought, Jason put his mind totally at ease and kept enjoying his book. Sarah certainly seemed deeply engrossed in her reading. Her sewing and patching had not stopped when the household was getting smaller and smaller, but it surely had been greatly reduced.

It was Sarah's personal policy to give each one of her children a quilt of her own making, of course, whenever that child got married. She did it for the boys and girls alike. All of the children now looked forward to getting one of their mother's beautifully pieced and hand-quilted quilts. Sarah said a long time ago, "My Jason, I can never stop quilting until all of our children are happily married."

He immediately asked her, "Why in the world do you say that, my Sarah?" She answered with, "Well, I hate to waste my quilting on a wasted son or daughter. Being in a bad marriage sure sounds like a waste to me. Don't think I'm crazy, but I could be. Maybe I just have not lived long enough to figure it out. By the time I get it figured out I could be dead." She laughed and laughed at her own wayward joke.

Jason said, "My Sarah, I think I get the meaning. Sometimes you are quite a deep thinker, and sometimes you are just a comedian. You leave us to figure it out."

Sarah got up from her chair, put her reading away, carefully marked. She put her hand on Jason's shoulder, kissed him on top of his big slightly balding head and said, "I'm off to make myself ready for bed. You coming?"

Jason said, "My Sarah, it's my bedtime too. Just stay awake until I get there. Did you hear me?"

Sarah chuckled and said, "Yes, my Jason, I sure can hear you." The cat was at the front door meowing, meowing to be let out into freedom. Jason opened the door and thought about freedom. Everything needs a certain amount of freedom, and it is used in different ways by different things. The cat needed to be free to go and relieve itself or just to see others more like itself or any number of other reasons. Jason remembered that quite a long time ago he had a "Solley Family Session" about the real meaning of freedom. He had been more than a little pleased with how the children seemed to have a pretty good knowledge of what freedom should do or not do in one's life. Well, so much for freedom. Jason quickly made himself ready for bed. He got into bed with his own Sarah. It was really a comforting thought.

It seemed like the roosters were crowing extra loud and the daylight was peeping in a little more than just bright. The Solleys had a good restful night. They realized in a little while that they had overslept. Without having to discuss it, both of them knew that this could become a very wonderful habit. They also knew that they had both earned the right to oversleep. They quickly put their feet to the floor (one on the right side and one on the left side of the bed).

Sarah knelt as usual beside the bed to say her prayers. Jason dressed quickly and made the fire in the cook stove.

Then he went to the barn where he found his favorite crib to say his morning prayers. From this time on, things moved along as usual in the early morning. Jason did not have any help with the barn work, and Sarah had no help in the house. This was all right. They thought of the early days of their marriage, and in some ways they could almost relive them. Quickly Sarah made the light fluffy biscuits to go with the cured ham slices, the scrambled eggs, home-made syrup, butter and milk. They didn't drink coffee every morning, but they did drink fresh buttermilk every day. Jason's nose seemed to guide him to the kitchen from the barn at the right time. The bucket of lukewarm water sat on the back porch table near the wash pan and the big bar of soap. Sarah kept clean home-made towels for ready continual use. There were still that row of towel hangers which held everybody's very own towel. Now there were only two towels hanging. The other part of the rack looked neglected and lonely. Only when some of the Solley children came home to visit did those empty towel places start to smile. Jason washed and rinsed his hands. Sarah had never relaxed her demands for certain aspects of cleanliness.

Jason, opening the kitchen door, said aloud, "Sarah, my Sarah, your kitchen has the smell that is making me real hungry! Where in the world are you?" Sarah did not answer immediately. Jason called again louder. She came dashing up the steps from the outhouse. She said, "Breakfast is ready and the table is set. I had an urgent call to our precious little house." That was the second name that the family had long ago given the outhouse. Jason said, "I didn't think of that. Well, you are here now and that's all that matters."

"Soon as I wash my hands I'll be right there," Sarah answered. They sat down to breakfast. It didn't seem to matter that the scrambled eggs had started to get cold. Sarah had pulled them far, far back on the stove because she didn't want them to keep cooking. They were not that bad. So the Solleys sat down and ate with enjoyment as usual. Sarah was thinking that her Jason had never been hard to please about his eating. Yet, she continued to believe that her cooking could stand some improvement. Then she said out loud, "My food has not been as good as my own ma, but it didn't yet kill any of the 15 of you." Then she laughed out loud.

Jason had always liked the way that Sarah could laugh at her own jokes. He said, "You know what? There were too many of us for you to kill off. So our stomachs just kept on getting tougher and tougher." Then he laughed before he quickly added, "You know your food has always been the best in Plum Creek Valley to me. If the children were here right now, they would all agree with that, I know."

Sarah sat up taller in her chair and said boldly, "Oh, yes, they sho' would agree with you just because they never got too many chances to eat the other people's food! The Solley table always had some kind of food on it when it was time to eat. So how in the world would they ever get the chance to find out? I guess maybe I'm glad they didn't so they kept thinking their mother was a good cook." At this, Sarah showed Jason how she really could laugh. She then got up and said, "These dishes sho' not going to get off the table by themselves. I think they looking right at me. I know they know you got plenty stuff to do in the corn, potato and peanut patches today."

Jason agreed, "Yes, I expect they do know that, but am I acting like I know it? So I guess I'd better get a move on me. You should not feed me so good. Make me lazy. Today I don't have any time to be lazy, not today."

Sarah said, "You soon forget your breakfast. Then you will work up the next meal. I've got to get to the mailbox for sure today. I need to write some letters real soon. I don't want to get behind with that. We will have more letters coming because we have had more and more children going away."

Jason said, "My Sarah, you got that just right."

"I do let you get away with leaving most of the letter writing to me. Of course, I really do enjoy it though. Also, you good about helping me wherever you can."

With that chit-chat done, the senior Solleys really got to their chores. There were many jobs that Sarah and Jason could now do less of because there were only two of them. Yet they always could benefit from having more than they needed because they could sell things in town.

After Sarah caught up with the churning, ironing and gathering vegetables, she looked again at the clock. If she got right to it, she could answer some letters and meet the mail carrier. Since they did not get their mail the day before, Sarah wanted to get the mail out of the box. She sat down with her writing tools and began to write as fast as she could think what to say next. She enjoyed writing these letters almost as much as she enjoyed getting them. When she was almost finished, she checked the clock again. Yes, if she hurried she would get there in time. Jason was no longer in the barn. He was doing some gathering outside of the barn in some of the patches. Sarah just pulled the front door closed and walked very swiftly down the road, carrying her stamps as well as the letters. She could always sit on the stomp if someone else had not beat her to it. If that happened, she would sit on the side of the road and lick her stamps for the letters.

Sarah found letters in the box from some of the children,

and she found some business letters from Jason's acquaintances, his lodge, the school board and the NAACP. Only one of the business letters included Sarah, and that was the one from the NAACP because she was also a great supporter of that truly amazing organization. She knew as well as Jason that Negroes especially needed this good group's efforts. They had made very sure that all of the Solley children were told by them about the need to be a part of this. Even the last three who were now away in school were aware of the works of this group. Two other neighbors had come to meet the mail carrier. After they chatted small friendly talk a little while, Sarah spotted the mail carrier coming. Those who had mail gave it to the mail carrier. Instead of putting the mail in their respective boxes, the carrier just handed each person her mail. Soon he was off again.

Sarah realized that she had a Sears and Roebuck Catalog among her pieces of mail. She would have a double good time when she got back to the house. She would read letters, and she would enjoy looking at the latest fashions in her Sears catalog. Sarah might end up stopping at the store when she was on a peddling trip. She would get some new yard goods and cut herself a newspaper pattern to make one of those pretty dresses. Maybe she'd make a wool suit and buy some shoes to match. After all, Hazel, who now worked as a show girl in Paris, France, had been saving up to give her and her Jason a trip to Paris. Sarah wanted to be ready for this trip for sure, and she thought about it very often. Sometimes she felt she could hardly wait.

As Sarah approached the house, she could see that Jason had returned. She called to him, "Jason! My Jason! When you get time, your mail is here."

"Anything worthwhile, you think?" he asked.

"Looks like a pretty good crop of mail to me," she answered.

"I'll be coming in pretty soon. Just want to finish this."

Sarah laid the mail on the little writing table and began to open and read the letters that had been left in the mailbox yesterday. She kept glancing at the catalog. Almost surely there would be something of interest in that big catalog. That thought reminded her again that Jason now had a full suit. In Paris there would be places to go where he would look so handsome. Sarah knew how proud of him that she was going to be. Of course, it seemed she was often proud of him.

For their midday meal Sarah opened a can of mackerel and made patties. She fried onions and potatoes together. Then she washed and peeled some late-ripening fresh peaches and reheated a few biscuits. This little meal was more than enough because they wanted to be sure to eat lightly now. Grandma Mattie, as all of the children fondly called Sarah's mother, had told them last Sunday at church to come for a "good ole" supper at her house today. Whenever they got that invitation, they let their mouths start watering. Mattie was in her 79th year. Her cooking just seem to get better. Sarah and Jason, as usual, worked with great anticipation all afternoon. When their night work had all been done, they washed their bodies, put on clean clothes, climbed into the wagon and rolled away to Mattie's.

Although Mattie Newsom knew the meaning of loneliness since Lawrence had that awful drowning accident that took him away from her forever, she still had been taken care of by her only daughter's family through the "Good Lawd in Heben." There had once been a widower who tried hard to be a second husband to her, but Mattie could never open her heart to him in that way. She knew that if Mattie Newsom could not open her heart to him, she could not open her bed to him. So, with that thought, Mattie let the widower be on about his way. From time to time they would talk and even laugh, but that was the end of that for them.

Jason, Sarah and Grandma Mattie enjoyed a good supper and plenty of laughing and talking. Although God did not give Mattie a son through birth, he still gave her the nicest son in the world, Jason. Mattie thought this thought every day and was thankful.

Mattie no longer lived in the Newsom home alone. She did for a short while. Then she was persuaded by a newlywed couple to let them share her home until at such time they could find a better arrangement. They came highly recommended. Mattie liked them right at first. The young woman, Minnie Walker, reminded her of her Sarah (sweet and smart, and so full of good manners). The young man, Arnold Walker, did not mind working. Mattie had been allowing them to work her land. They expressed a desire to save their money and perhaps buy Mattie's house and land. They were good prospects, and things went well between them all. Mattie had never regretted her decision.

As the Solleys rode back to their own house, they were sitting pretty close to each other on the spring seat. They were full of good chicken and dumplings, sage sausage cornbread dressing, mustard greens, cucumber pickles and plum pudding. They were a contradiction at that special moment.

Sarah was the first to break the silence. She said very quietly, "I am happy and yet I am sad. I wonder if you feel what I am feeling at this moment."

Jason had no need to ask her what she was feeling. He knew exactly what she was feeling because he was feeling it, too. So Jason let loose one hand from the reins, touched

Sarah's hand ever so lightly. Then he looked into her eyes and said, "Grandma Mattie is always happy to make a good dinner or supper for us. Yet there is a void that you and me just can't fill. We see that, and we are sad for her, and for ourselves when that day arrives. We know that our day will come. This is the way of the world. This is the way of God. Is this what you were feeling, my Sarah?"

Sarah was overflowing with love for his man whom she had loved for just over 40 years. He knew her too well. She could not have expressed this feeling as well as he did, but he had said everything exactly right. Now she tried to speak, but her heart was filling her mouth. She fought back the tears of joy and sadness. Then she said to herself, "My, my, don't be such a baby, Sarah." She said aloud, "I do love you more than my life, Jason."

He said, "Again, we are feeling the very same thing. Aren't we blessed, my beautiful sweet Sarah?" The mules must have felt the mood because they had slowed down almost to a stop. Jason reminded them to step it up with his "Gidda yup, gidda yup," as he shook the reins. They understood to pick up speed and go on home. The wagon moved faster and faster until it came to a stop at the Solley house. Jason helped Sarah down from the wagon. She thanked him and actually ran into the house. Why she had the urge to run instead of just walking was not so obvious even to her. It could be that after leaving Jason's side in the wagon she needed the security of their home. Those few words in the wagon were big little words or little big words. One could think either way on that, she guessed.

Sarah had always greeted her mother with a tight hug, and they left each other with very tight hugs. She had admired her mother across the table because again she was remembering that she learned to love from her. She learned to respect from her. She learned to care about others from her. She had to also include her daddy in all of this, even though she was with her mother more hours in the day. It was her daddy who was always, in his quieter way, showing her so much love and giving her his total support. Yes, she sure had been blessed real big. It had seemed a shame almost that she had had no one to share all of this with. She guessed things did finally even out because she had 14 children to her mother's one. The large number made room for much sharing and much growing.

Jason had come in from unhitching the team and wagon. Both could settle down for the day. This time was always a good time when busy people can just stop being busy for a while. Sarah and Jason thought of the young Walkers often because they were the kind of people that Mattie could trust in her house and on her farm. Mattie always seemed perfectly happy with these young marrieds sharing her home. The Solleys prepared for bed. Then they read for a while.

The Sullivan Murder Case

The Amy Sullivan Murder case did not die after Claude went away to school. Claude, though only 15 at the time, had a theory about the murder. Amy's husband John was a respected businessman in Plum Creek Valley. His wife Amy had been a thriving dress shop owner, who might or might not spend much time in the shop. Sometimes she would take trips to larger cities like Dallas, St. Louis or Chicago to buy. Amy Sullivan was well dressed, college educated and extremely attractive. Naturally, there were many questions when she was found dead in their home, shot to death while her husband was away on business. Claude had speculated that just maybe this nice wife was not as nice as everyone was led to believe. Jason had been surprised to see his young unassuming son think this way, because such a thing was possible, but Claude was so young.

Every time Jason's paper came, he looked for and read with full attention the write-up on the Amy Sullivan case. Sarah was just as interested as Jason. Amy Sullivan had been good to the women folk of the Solley family. It seems that as the story unfolded, Amy had been possibly involved with a lover who had a jealous wife. The wife was under suspicion because she had owned a gun of the kind that Amy Sullivan had been killed with. The murderer had been very careful to wear gloves or wipe away fingerprints. The case was the talk of not only Plum Creek Valley, but it extended far into the deep South and also to other parts of the United States. The case was becoming more and more difficult for law officials to figure out. It was getting to be one of the foremost murder crimes of the area. Jason and Sarah saved all of the articles regarding this case for Claude to read especially, not only because of his youthful theory about the murder, but because of his desire to study law.

As time went on,, the case became more and more difficult to solve. By Christmas there had not been a break in the case. The three younger children took full advantage of their holiday break and came home from their schools. Claude was especially glad that his parents had taken him seriously enough about the desire to be a lawyer to save all of the stories about the murder case. He became more determined than before.

All of the children came home for Christmas Day except Hazel who lived in Paris. Some drove their cars, some came on the train, and some came by Greyhound Bus. Most of them came on Christmas Eve and left the day after Christmas. Those who were no longer living at home divided their sleeping time between Grandma Mattie's house and Jason and Sarah's house. Grandma Mattie cooked all of the delicious sweet potato pies, baked several hens, and fried several pullets. She also made cornbread and sage-sausage dressing. Sarah cooked cured ham, made collard greens, corn pudding with bacon bits, and home-made apple sauce. Jason made several pans of his famous Plum Creek Valley crackling bread. The feast of the Solleys and Grandma Mattie was on. Everybody had a wonderful time. This was a time nobody would soon forget. It was special.

This was a slave-born four-generation celebration. Mattie

Newsom or Grandma Mattie born 1860, daughter Sarah born 1879, granddaughter Nona born 1901, great-grandson Joe Jr. born 1921. Joe Baker, Jr. and his parents were proud because he was Grandma Mattie's very first great-grandchild. Many might come after, but none came before, and Grandma Mattie stood up from the improvised oversized Christmas dinner table. She clapped her hands exactly five times and said, "Very soon I'm a'gonna be 80 years old. My husband, Grandpa Lawrence, got 'drownded' when that old Plum Creek rose so high and so wide that it just washed away the bridge, it washed away my Lawrence, it washed away the buggy and mule. The Good Lawd let me stand here and be leading four generations that started before us colored people got to be free from slavery. Abraham Lincoln did this when I was five years. I am here to tell it today."

"Grandma Mattie, can you tell us how old Grandpa Lawrence was when he became an ex-slave?" Edward, the youngest Solley, asked.

Grandma Mattie very proudly stood a little taller as she answered, "I sho' can! He was two years older than me. He was seven when Mr. Lincoln let us go free in 1865. But I mean really free."

Edward said, "Well, I must say that I for one am very glad that it happened. Yet, I can see places where we need to be more free."

Jason said, "Could I ask a question, Edward?"

Edward had always, since he was real young, noticed that his daddy liked to ask his children questions. The older Solley children would try to see which one could give a very good answer. If their daddy seemed really pleased with the answer, everything was good. So Edward responded to Jason by saying, "Yes, Daddy, please ask your question. Maybe now that I have been going off to high school I might give a more suitable answer. Let me have your question right now." Edward looked pleased.

Jason asked, "Where are some of the places that we could use more freedom? Just name two for me." Now that was the way of Jason.

Everybody else knew to keep quiet for the moment. This was Edward's time and Edward was the very youngest Solley. Edward thought pretty quickly. Then he said, "If we were more free, Claude and I would not have to go away on the Greyhound bus to high school. There would be one for us closer. That is my number one. Number two is there wouldn't be so many Negroes still in the field picking King Cotton when they should be in King School. Yes, cotton's got good reasons to be the King to some white people, but I bet you cannot find one single Negro who would agree!"

Jason was smiling. Everybody was smiling because Edward came through. Jason said, "I am satisfied with your places where we could use more freedom."

Sarah said to Mattie, "Well, Ma, it seems that you got something started pretty good."

Mattie smiled and said, "I sho' do likes to git good stuff started. When these 'grans' and their daddies and mamas get started, I do likes to listen real hard. I don't want to miss nothing of this. No, no!"

With Christmas dinner over, dishes all washed, and leftover food stored, the big family just enjoyed each for a while longer.

It was Edward who now had a real special announcement for everybody. He thought it was special, and he was ready to share it with this big family. He just said quite suddenly, "I know I have a long time to wait. I have a whole lot of studying to do, I'll need some good scholarships and everything.

One day I'm going to be the best doctor in these whole United States of America." Everybody looked on admiringly.

Jim, the oldest Solley brother who now worked for the railroad company, was overjoyed to hear his baby brother thinking this way. It made him feel good. So he spoke strongly, and he said very loudly, "Baby brother, if you really do want to be a doctor, you can count on me to help you. It's good you are letting me know so early so that I can start to put a savings box up for you."

Everybody was interested. A little first year high school country Negro boy thinking big thoughts, and he shared them. Before anyone else could make a statement, Claude looked first at his two parents and said, "They already know that I am going to be a lawyer and take on the real hard cases like the Amy Sullivan."

Jim said to Claude, "My second baby brother will get some help from me too. It's just good that you both are making your announcements early." Then one by one the older Solley children promised their support to the baby boys. Jason and Sarah were feeling really happy about their children's good intentions. Just before they all sat down to dinner, family prayer was said. Now it was time to say good-night prayers. Everybody held hands and Jason gave thanks again. Grandma Mattie got hugged almost to death, but she did not mind one bit. Some of the children would be leaving next morning. Others would leave in the afternoon. By nightfall the day after Christmas every one except the two high schoolers had left for their homes. That was a never-to-be-forgotten Christmas.

Claude and Edward had slept soundly and awakened ready to help Jason with the farm animals and then go visiting. Some of their friends had been away to different high schools. Some did not get off to high school yet, but helped care for their families. They sawed and cut up firewood for selling in town, as well as home use. Jason and Sarah felt sad for the children who didn't get to go off to high school right away, because they knew that some would never go. That was the saddest part of it all. They would try to encourage these children by making statements to them which demonstrated loving concern. Claude and Edward sawed firewood, too, while they were home for Christmas vacation, but they knew that soon they would be on the Greyhound Bus to Sampson High School in Tolletville. The older Solley children did not have to be told by their parents to always remember the young sisters and brothers. That was just the right way to do it, and it was the Solley way.

One day shortly after Christmas, Sarah came bursting in from the mailbox with the paper. She said, "Look y'all! Look y'all!"

Jason said, "What on God's green earth is the matter, my Sarah?"

Sarah answered breathlessly, "It seems like the police and the detectives have made a real break-through in the Amy Sullivan case!"

Claude stopped stacking firewood by the fireplace. Edward stopped washing dishes, and Jason stopped shelling dry peas. All of them had turned their eyes toward the paper in Sarah's hand. It seemed at that moment nobody was looking at Sarah, only at the paper in her hand. She handed the paper to Jason, of course. Claude looked as though he was about to snatch it from his daddy. Jason surprised everybody by handing the paper over to the future lawyer. Claude read the news story. Then he said very excitedly, "Mrs. Sullivan was not killed by a jealous wife of her lover! She was killed by Mr. Sullivan because he found out about this other man who Mrs.

Sullivan was seeing behind his back. It seems like Mr. Sullivan meant to kill the man, but accidentally killed his wife. Oh, how terrible! How terrible!" They all looked at Claude.

Jason said, "Well, Claude, do you still want to study law and defend people like John Sullivan?"

Claude said, "More than ever I want to study law."

Edward just said, "Keep that in mind as we ride the bus back to school."

Sophie did not get to stay home after Christmas as the young boys had done. She had a job on the Howard campus which she needed to get back to. Sophie was enjoying college very much, even though she sometimes held down two part-time jobs, one on campus and one off campus in a department store. The one on campus was a work-study job. She never saw the pay, but it was applied to her account. The other job supplied her small change for items of necessity. Sophie didn't mind being busy as long as she had sufficient time to keep her grades high. That, she knew, was a must.

Even though Louise was a Howard University graduate and now an English teacher in one of the D.C. high schools, she did not allow little sister Sophie to believe she could just skate through. For work had been good for Louise. It would be good for her baby sister who was ten years her junior. Louise loved her little sister very much, but she did not allow herself to contribute to her weakness.

The day came around faster than Claude and Edward could imagine to go to that bus station. They had enjoyed the time at home getting to know their daddy better, and getting to love their mother Sarah and Grandma Mattie more. Edward had been thinking a lot. He said, "When I get to be a doctor, maybe I'll find a way to make sweet people like mine live a long, long time."

New Year, New Telephone, Travel Time

Christmas came and Christmas left. Now a new year had found its way into the Solleys' life. It came bringing joy and happiness. Charley, the fourth son and the sixth child of Jason and Sarah, had a serious ax accident as he chopped wood when he was still a youngster. The doctor had said that the availability and quick use of a white neighbor's telephone had saved his life. Jason knew that Alexander Graham Bell's invention, two years after his birth in 1877, was something that he would like to have. He also knew that it was not near a priority. There were too many urgent needs ahead of it. The children knew this. But the one child who knew that one day he would do something about this was Charley. The time had come with this new year of 1940.

Without Jason's knowledge, Charley arranged to have a telephone ordered and placed in the Solley home. Jason did not have to make payments for its monthly use. Charley loved and respected his daddy and just wanted to do this little thing for a man who gave so much, but asked for so little in return. At last, Jason walked into his house, after a pre-arranged trip to town, and found what else? A telephone and a little book with names, addresses and phone numbers. This gesture might have been small for Charley, now a railroad man, but it was a grand gesture for farmer Jason Solley. Sarah, who had been sworn to secrecy, helped Charley living in Pennsylvania to set everything up. Now she was happier and more excited than Jason, if such a thing were possible. Jason was totally surprised and extremely pleased with Charley's gift.

That very same day Jason sat down to write a letter of thanks to Charley. It was only after he had painstakingly written Charley's letter that he thought that maybe he could have called him on their new telephone. Just maybe? Maybe? He would have to find out all about that sort of thing later. He and Sarah were going to enjoy their brand new telephone. Some people did not have telephones, naturally. So they could not talk to them, naturally. But until then they would use their telephone just when they needed to.

Sarah walked around the house looking toward her Jason and smiling to herself. Then she said aloud, "My Jason, how do you feel now that you can talk on a white man's talking device? You once said that seemed like progress and you wanted to progress."

Jason smiled. Then he said, "Oh, my Sarah. We have to start now, today, and never again think of the telephone or anything else as the white man's as long as we own one ourselves. Let us remember that this is ours. Our son paid for it. Our son will see to it that for the rest of our lives we'll be able to talk on it. So this is *our* talking device, and we must *always* think of it this way until we die."

Sarah could see how serious her Jason was. She would remember. She answered, "You are right, my Jason. It belongs to us. She reached for his hand. They looked at each other and smiled a warm, warm smile.

Tomorrow Sarah or Jason would go to the mailbox. Two important pieces of mail might be handled. First was the telephone "Thanks" letter. Second was the letter that their

"Dreamer" Hazel was sending with their tickets to visit her in Paris. Sarah was getting more excited by the day. Hazel had been saving up to give them this trip of their lifetime, and had arranged for them to see her out on the big brightly lighted stage dancing, singing and just generally performing. Sarah just knew that they were going to enjoy this very special treat. The more she thought about it, the faster Sarah's heart was beating. She turned to Jason and said, "Jason, my Jason, I can hardly wait for the mail carrier tomorrow. Maybe you should go to get the mail." Sarah did have a child-like quality.

Jason looked at his wife, and then he answered, "I agree with you that I should go. If the letter comes from Hazel, you'll be too excited. If it doesn't come tomorrow, I'm afraid you'll be too disappointed. Either way might not be the best for you. So I'll go. You just finish making your pretty suit that you intend to travel in on that big airplane. We'll probably get that letter tomorrow. If not tomorrow, the next day." Their tickets arrived the following day. All was well. Sarah agreed that she should finish her sewing.

They had gone to town and bought a suitcase and a very large pocketbook for Sarah. Jason traveled each year to his Masonic Lodge meeting. However, that was never overseas. He now needed a small bag for his personal things just in case his big grip did not arrive on the same airplane that he did. He had said to Sarah that Hazel reminded them to pack what they would have to use immediately in a small hand-carried bag. They were both trying to follow her very explicit directions. Hazel realized that her parents had never had such a grand trip as this one. She did so want everything to go smoothly for them while they traveled to Paris. Once they arrived, she would be in charge of them. Hazel had told the

217

other Solley children who were in a financial position to help, that she wanted them to remember their parents for spending money. She was taking care of tickets, food and lodging. The Solley children again came through. They believed sincerely that their parents had always loved them enough to make big sacrifices for them. Now it was their turn. Therefore, Jason and Sarah didn't have to just depend on the meager "bank" behind the bed savings. All they needed to do was make proper arrangements for their home to be cared for while they were gone.

Jason asked Gerald, his farmer son, to come over daily to see about the farm animals. Since it was not yet plowing or planting time, there would be no need for field work to be done. It was early spring. Sarah had arranged for Grandma Mattie to stay in their house while they went to Paris. Mattie's nice tenants, Arnold and Minnie Walker, promised to take good care of her place and also to come over to Sarah and Jason's sometimes. This was a perfect arrangement. The Solleys could relax and enjoy their trip abroad. They knew they could depend on Gerald and Grandma Mattie. Gerald knew he could depend on his wife Nancy to help in any way she could. Nancy really cared for both of her husband's parents. She considered them to be her parents, too. They had always treated her that way. She highly respected them.

The packing time had arrived. Sarah had made very sure that Jason's shirts were perfectly done, his underwear and socks were clean and ready. Jason pressed his black pin-striped suit, for sure. He, of course, pressed his other extra pants and jacket. Carefully he packed. He somehow felt the need to be more careful for this special trip with his Sarah. They were going to not just ride the train this time, but fly on an airplane! Now Jason was getting excited, too. Sarah felt Jason's

PLUM CREEK VALLEY

quiet excitement as she went hustling and bustling about her own packing. Oh, yes, she had sewed some, but Hazel had promised to take her and Jason for a tiny shopping spree. Hazel wanted both her parents to enjoy their trip to Paris, France, and to go home with something for each and something for Grandma Mattie, for sure.

When Hazel had arrived in Paris four years before, she was exactly 21 years old, directly from New York City, indirectly from Plum Creek Valley. She was a deep South country girl, turned New York City girl. She had revised many of her ways of doing things, but tried hard not to revise her basic thinking. This was the reason that she had survived in beautiful Paris. There were temptations beyond her wildest dreams. Yet, Hazel had survived, and not only survived, but had done exceedingly well. Sometimes she would feel just like pinching herself to see if she was awake and know this young woman really did have two wonderful parents in Plum Creek Valley, Arkansas, U.S.A. Hazel knew at those particular times that it had been her mother, Sarah, and her daddy, Jason, who had given her the ability and the encouragement to think straight strong thoughts. Hazel realized in Paris, France, just as she had learned in New York City, that people were still basically people, and that men were still men. She was not only talented, but quite attractive. Grandma Mattie had not minced any words of advice or encouragement. She had aspired to remember all of those straightforward words that Grandma Mattie had spoken so plainly. She honestly believed that so many times she might have gotten herself in over her head, so to speak, if her Grandma had not lovingly drilled and poured certain facts into her head. So when she thought of her parents she also had to give her grandma credit.

Hazel had been diligent in her pursuit of the ability to

learn and speak fluently the French language. She had not missed any of the cues she had been given for learning. By the time she planned to see her parents again, she hoped they would be totally impressed. The best part of this was that she'd be able to cope with living in a city she had learned to love. Hazel planned to greet her parents a first and second time. The first time she would do it in the only language they spoke, English. The second greeting would be a fun greeting, French. She knew she could quickly teach them both to greet the French and to thank the French. They were still very alert, she was thinking. So on their first day she would tell them how to say, "Good day" or "Bonjour." Then she would go on to "Good evening" or "Bonsoir." There would be one more and that is "Thank you" or "Merci beaucoup." She planned to stop her French lesson with her parents at that. Hazel knew they'd be thrilled to interact in even a limited way with their host countrymen. Oh, yes, she was getting excited all over again. It had started when she knew for sure that she would be able to pull it off. All of her friends and co-workers knew that Hazel Solley would have very distinguished visitors from the U.S.A., her very own parents. They were anxious to greet them.

The elder Solleys were many miles across the country and across the Atlantic ocean doing their own kind of thinking and making preparations for this first time in a lifetime trip. They, of course, talked a lot to each other.

Jason came in from the barn and called to Sarah, "My Sarah, my Sarah!" She didn't answer. Jason called again louder, "Sarah, my Sarah, where are you?"

Sarah came rushing in from the potato house inside the garden. She said, "How long have you been calling me? I was down in the garden cellar." The garden cellar was a cistern-like opening inside a small one-room house in the garden. There were several steps with a substantial banister leading down onto the floor. There it was, a great storage place for all kinds of things which needed to be kept for a while without canning or curing. They kept sweet potatoes, Irish potatoes, sun-dried onions, etc. It was difficult to hear down there. Family members never went down there to remain but a few minutes at a time, and then it was not until some other family member was close by. Of course, there were times when something was needed to use in meal preparation and no one else was near. It was "Jason's law" that when that happened just wait. Colored women were especially supposed to be careful about this for fear of getting "caught" down in the cellar where almost anything imaginable might happen.

Sarah was in for a reprimanding from her Jason. She hurriedly said, "I needed some onions for my stew. I was only down there for just a couple of minutes, my Jason." She almost fearfully waited for Jason's response. It was not because he would ever do anything to hurt her, but he was very protective of her. He had been the same way about the six girls. Now that there were only two of them in the house again, he felt the need for Sarah to adhere to this old unwritten rule. He couldn't bear to have anything unusual and unnecessary happen to his Sarah.

Jason said aloud, "I was thinking that I want you to be careful about that garden cellar. Please don't go down in it if I am not in the house or on the back porch, please."

Sarah answered very lovingly, "Oh my Jason, my Jason, you do take such good care of me. I do know what you mean. I promise to remember this always. Thank you for looking after me."

Jason answered, "I know you will, my Sarah. If you don't, you will be in deep trouble with me." After this conversation they looked toward the meal that Sarah was preparing. They would eat and then call it a day, after the dishes were done, of course. Both looked forward to just relaxing and reading a little.

The time was getting closer and closer to Gerald, Nancy and Grandma Mattie taking over the care of this Solley place. Gerald would not only do the feeding and watering of the farm animals, he would do the milking as well. Nancy would help with gathering eggs and feeding the chickens. The churning of milk, cleaning out ashes, etc., Grandma Mattie could easily do. She had been insisting that she really didn't need all of this "babying." She loudly protested, "I've been doing all of this for so many years! Why do I need so much help now? Y'all sho' don't think I'm that decrepit, now do ya? Answer me, Jason!"

Jason always knew just the right thing to say to his dear mother-in-law. He would simply pat her and kindly say, "Grandma Mattie, there is no way we could call you anything except the good cooking, pretty sewing and quilting, straight talking, sweet woman that you are. Is that answer good enough for the mother of the woman I love?" Grandma Mattie satisfied, would answer, "I reckon so."

The Solleys were glad that they had another Sunday before it was time to take off on their trip abroad. That Sunday promised to be happily filled. It was a day of loving pampering for Jason and Sarah. Their dear friends wanted to step in on the bon voyage. Catherine Kelly, Sarah's oldest and best friend, and her husband still lived in Tall Point. They had three sons all living in Little Rock. These two women had not only courted their fellas about the same time, but they had been there like maid and matron of honor for each other when they were married. Sarah married two months before Catherine in

1898. Catherine's first son was born in 1899. Sarah's first girl came along the following year, 1900. The two friends often laughed together about the way their babies came. Catherine's babies started to come a little earlier than Sarah's, but Sarah's babies, once they found the way out, just kept pouring out. There was no stopping them. As these two friends laughed, they remained grateful for their husbands and their children. Both had always had similar values, and their husbands didn't mind working. Sarah had always remained busy enough without going outside of the yard to work. On the other hand, Catherine had worked as a cook while her boys were trying to get educated beyond one-room school. This had worked out well. Now she was at home just like Sarah. She had a telephone, too. They could talk on the phone.

Catherine and her husband had invited Sarah and her husband to Sunday dinner after church. They picked them up in their black Ford, and after dinner and visiting together, they would return the Solleys to their home. This would be the last time they would see each other before that "Big Bird" flew off with them to Paris. Catherine was excited for her dearest friend. Dinner was really special. Since Catherine had worked as a cook in the Tall Point Hotel, she used her expertise to cook more than her everyday fare. She made beef roast with potatoes, onions and carrots, green beans seasoned with cured ham bits, pecan pies. And, of course, she made home-made dinner rolls. There was plenty of very good fresh lemonade. When the Solleys entered the house, everything was smelling so good!

Jason spoke first to Catherine and said, "Even if I had just eaten and was full to the brim, these good smells would still make me hungry! I'm afraid you won't have much left for eating later when I get through!"

Sarah chimed in, "I'm afraid all of this good food will make us lose our manners, Catherine. You'll forgive us since you know that you'll be the cause of it."

Everybody laughed. Catherine's husband David added, "We're just happy for you to take this special trip, and we're glad we can be just a little part of this. Maybe next time Catherine and I can go, too. Oh, I see how everybody is looking at me (just like I'm not serious, but I am serious). Ex-slaves' grandchildren can now start doing a little more about getting out of these United States of America. Your daughter Hazel has proved to us all that this can go on. Do you see what I mean?" Everybody looked straight at David and knew that he was not merely chit-chatting now.

Catherine responded first, "I do see what you mean, David, and if any of us here know that you are serious, it is I, your wife, 'cause you don't spare mere words." Catherine knew her husband.

Jason said, "This sounds like my Sarah and I will be inviting you and Catherine to our home for a pre-overseas traveling dinner. Wouldn't that be just fantastic?"

Catherine smiled a great big smile as she said, "Well, I can hardly wait."

These four friends sat around after dinner for a while longer just talking and laughing. Whenever they got together, it was so special. Catherine did not do the dishes while she had company. Not a single precious minute would be wasted. So dishes could just wait.

Sarah reached over to lightly touch Jason's knee. Then she said aloud to Catherine and David, "We have just had the best time and ate the really good dinner. Now we should go home and let you get back to clean up our mess. Isn't it awful that you wouldn't let me help you clean up the kitchen! Now you have to come home and do this."

Catherine said, "I did it the way I wanted to do it, my friend Sarah. You and Jason just go get your night work done. That will be a'plenty. We'll do what needs to be done here. No help is required from the Solleys." The men did not interfere in their wives' discussion and settlement of the situation.

Jason stood up and made a small speech. He said, "When good friends love you enough to prepare a wonderful dinner for you, and then encourage you to eat way too much, and before that come and get you, then load you up in their car and take you home again, these are strictly good friends. My Sarah and I could not have expected this kind of treatment if we had been Mr. Franklin D. Roosevelt. I bet he was not treated in the White House today the way we were treated in our good friends Catherine's and David's home. This is not a statement to say how good we are, but to say how good our hostess and host are. We do thank you, and we do love you so very much."

With those words said, he looked straight at Sarah, who immediately knew what to do next. She stood as close beside Jason as she possibly could. They applauded and applauded. The women hugged each other like the old true friends they were. The men shook hands and patted each other on the back. They got ready to go to the car. The men assisted the women into the car, and off they went to the country.

As they drove along, everybody was perhaps subconsciously looking for every sign of spring that might be showing forth. Jason and Sarah knew that they would make their trip and return before the spring farm activities required their immediate attention. David was a very smooth and cautious driver. Therefore, everyone enjoyed the ride. Catherine had quickly and unobtrusively packed a little basket of supper from her leftovers. When she handed the basket to Sarah, she was saying and laughing, "Take this because you two won't be feeling as full later on as you think you are feeling right now. Jason will probably be just starving to death. You were not supposed to cook today. So here is a bite for both you."

Catherine had taken her guests by total surprise. They didn't know when she'd had time to do this. Sarah thought that there was not much like this which could get by her. Catherine surely must have packed that basket in advance. She didn't tell, but just pleased her friend by smiling.

When they were crossing over the Plum Creek Valley bridge, Sarah thought of her daddy again. She guessed that she never crossed without remembering his tragic death in that buggy. She would not allow herself to feel sadness today. She would keep remembering all of the quiet and wonderful ways that he had. She would remember how they could work together since he had no sons. She worked with him while he always remembered that she was still a girl. Sarah quickly brought her thoughts back to the present, back to her husband and her friends in their car. Next thing she knew, they were driving up in front of her own house. David came around to help her from the car. She reached over and kissed her friend Catherine, who handed her a little coin purse, saying, "Buy yourself something as pretty as your are in Paris. Then think of me, my friend."

Sarah was totally surprised and, oh, so, so pleased. She had not thought of getting anything else today from her dear friend. Her eyes glazed over with wetness and tears started to roll down her cheeks. Sarah said, "Thank you. Oh, thank you so very much."

Catherine simply said, "My dear friend, I wish I could do more for you. Have a great trip and give Hazel nine hugs for me." With that, Catherine laughed. They all waved "goodbye" as David turned the car around and they headed toward Tall Point and home.

Sarah and Jason said to each other that they had enjoyed their friends and all this day. They changed their Sunday clothes and did their night work. It wouldn't be long before Gerald and Nancy and Grandma Mattie would take over for about nine days. Their tickets were in the drawer and their suitcases were almost ready. Everything was falling very nicely into the right places. Jason fed the barn animals, milked the cows and fed the chickens. Sarah gathered the eggs and churned the milk. Both of the Solleys knew how to move quickly to get everything done. They would finish, then sit down, read and completely relax. The day had been, oh, so good to them. What more could they ask the Good Lord for right now.

Just as they closed the doors, the telephone rang. They thought most likely it was one of the children who now had telephones. It was Gerald. He said that he was just checking to make sure he and Nancy had the time right for them to pick up Grandma Mattie to bring her to stay in their house. Also the time that he should be ready to take them to get the train to Little Rock to board their flight to New York and then Paris, France. They would be able to rest easy about this trip because Gerald, Nancy and Grandma Mattie were as solid as a rock. They would take good care of everything.

Jason was thinking about Grandma Mattie's being a caretaker of their home. It would have been wonderful if her first great-grandson, Joe Baker, Jr., could have been close enough to hear first hand some of the occurrences in these United States of America that she had witnessed. Over the span of her years since 1860, she had witnessed ex-slaves' families vote, use the telephones, ride in motor cars, attend colleges, write books, buy birth control, witness the Roaring '20s, terrible influenza epidemic, World War I, Great Depression, Ku Klux Klan, Madam C.J. Walker's Hair Care, ride in airplanes, establish the NAACP, pay poll tax to vote, live with Jim Crow Laws, etc. It was a good thing that her first great-grandson could not be near her right now simply because this ex-slave's great-grandchild was away attending college. Yes, college!! Grandma Mattie could only dream of such a thing when she was that age. Maybe she did not even dream of it. Yet it is happening now and she cannot just smile, she can laugh loudly.

Jason laughed happily and said, "Sarah, my dear Sarah, don't think your Jason has completely lost his mind."

She answered, "I just thought something or other had got you tickled. I says to myself that it had to be good. Then I thought you could have just been thinking about your Sarah." Then she laughed. He said, "This time it was about Grandma Mattie. I was thinking of some of the things this little slave born girl had lived to see in her life. Of course, I don't have to tell you how often you make me laugh every day after more than 40 years. I love you more each day. If I make you mad, it is always my aim to make you smile at me again. I couldn't ever stand for you to be out of sorts with me. But you know that." Sarah was overcome with these meaningful sweet sentiments. She flew into Jason's arms. They hugged each other just like they had just married. "Oh my Jason, it has only gotten better. We've always worked out anything and everything. I do love you with all my heart!"

Now Jason could just get out the words "Me, too, my Sarah. Me, too!"

Tomorrow would be the Big Day to travel on that Big Bird. Jason and Sarah went to bed early because Gerald would drop Grandma Mattie off early. The packing had been made complete, including three precious pieces of reading items for the plane ride. They were the *Holy Bible, Up from Slavery* by Booker T. Washington, the great Negro leader/writer, and the poem *The Creation* by another great Negro writer/songwriter, James Weldon Johnson. These were packed in their hand-carried bags so that they'd always have access to them while traveling.

The Solleys had slept extremely well for two such excited people. They arose and were ready to go when Gerald came with Grandma Mattie. It was the middle of March, and they both felt like it was fully spring. Everybody moved fast. It was a busy time. There was a whole lot of hugging and kissing. The bags were loaded into the car as Sarah and Jason climbed in. Gerald quickly rolled away to the train. The oldest daughter, Susan, who now lived in Little Rock, met them at their train, carried them to the airport, and watched their plane fly off to New York for the Paris flight. She didn't want to stop hugging her beloved parents, but she did. Susan was so happy for two deserving people. In New York they had no time to waste, and this was just fine with them. They quickly boarded their plane, found their seats, buckled up, and waited to hear those famous words again, "This is your captain speaking …"

THE END